ADVENTURE
STORIES FOR
BOYS

ADVENTURE
STORIES FOR
BOYS

Written by Nicola Baxter   **Illustrated by Colin King and Ken Morton**

ARMADILLO

ISBN 978-1-84322-455-6

3 5 7 9 10 8 6 4 2

Published by Armadillo Books
An imprint of Bookmart Limited
Registered Number 2372865
Trading as Bookmart Ltd
Blaby Road, Wigston
Leicestershire, LE18 4SE
England

This material was taken from the following titles
previously published by Bookmart Ltd
The Perils of Pirates and Other Dastardly Deeds
The Disasters of Dragons and Other Fiery Fiascos
Giants Ogres & Trolls

Printed in Thailand

CONTENTS

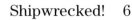

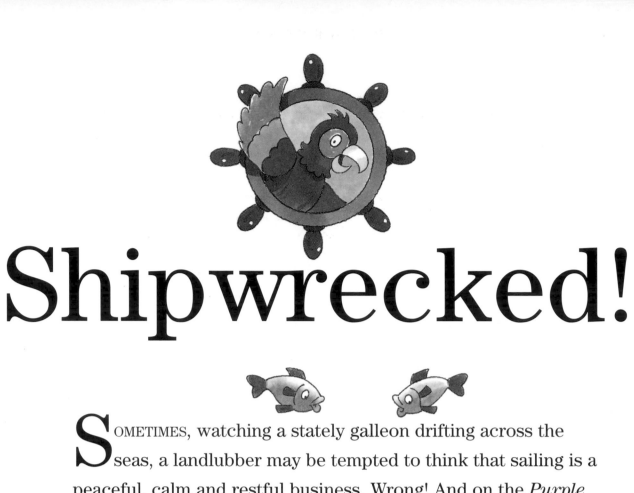

Shipwrecked!

SOMETIMES, watching a stately galleon drifting across the seas, a landlubber may be tempted to think that sailing is a peaceful, calm and restful business. Wrong! And on the *Purple Pimple*, commanded by Pugnacious Pete the Pirate, very, very wrong!

There is creaking (of timbers and Pete's wooden leg) and cursing and clattering and clammering. There are sails that snap and a parrot that squawks. It is not the kind of ship you would choose for a leisurely cruise.

On the particular day when we catch up with Pugnacious Pete and his motley crew, there is an even bigger noise. It goes something like this:

GuUUhaSChAM!

No, it's not Pugnacious Pete sneezing or Poisonous Pedro (the parrot) attacking the cabin boy. It's the *Purple Pimple* bashing into an unsuspecting island. For a pirate, Pugnacious Pete's sailing skills leave a lot to be desired. But it will not surprise you to learn that, as he picks himself up off the deck, the mean mariner is not blaming *himself* for the disaster. Suddenly the ship is very empty and the island is very crowded.

"Who," roars Pete, red in the face, "is supposed to be steering this ship?"

Pete's miserable crew knows better than to point out the obvious, which is that Pete himself was at the helm. Poisonous Pedro has no such inhibitions. He squawks the fact loudly into Pete's right ear and then, for good measure, repeats the message in his left ear. Pete's ears haven't seen soap and water for many moons, but that's not the kind of thing that bothers Pedro. His own hygiene would horrify his dear old mother back in Borneo.

Pugnacious Pete pauses only for a second. There's no way he can believe this is his fault. His vile voice rings out once more.

"Who," he demands, "is the unfathomable idiot who put this island here?" (Actually, those are not his exact words. I'm having to clean up Pete's language so as not to offend delicate adults—you know what I mean.)

Well, even Pedro doesn't have an answer to that one, so Pete stomps down the gangplank to view the damage.

The *Purple Pimple* could do with a coat of paint. Several repairs are needed. It is not the most beautiful boat on the seven seas. But none of this is because it just collided with an inoffensive island. Amazingly, the collision has done very little damage.

Pugnacious Pete grunts and gurgles a bit, but even he's relieved. There doesn't seem to be much of a problem.

Twenty minutes later, a thought filters through to Pete's brain. "You snivelling shipworms," he says to his crew, "we've got a problem. Can any of you excuses for sailors tell me what it is?"

The sailors try hard not to catch Pete's eye. They all know what the problem is, but no one wants to be the one to say it. Only the cabin boy isn't yet as scared of Pete as he should be.

"We're stuck," he says. "We can't shift the ship."

Pugnacious Pete looks around for something to throw at the cabin boy. That's just the way bad news takes him. As there's not much on the island except a couple of palm trees and a surprised snake or two, Pete looks in vain. In exasperation, he pulls off his wooden leg and smacks the cabin boy smartly around the ears with it—before falling flat on his face.

It's not long before conditions on the island go
from bad to worse. There's no fresh water,
so the crew is obliged to drink the
Purple Pimple's rum rations.
It doesn't do a bit of good to
their brains or their brawn.
As the sun goes down, the
crew reaches a state of
massive marine misery.

"We're all going to die!"
booms the bosun in
tones of doom.

"First we'll shrivel,"
sobs the ship's cook,
who knows more
than he should
about death by
misadventure.

"I wish I'd been nicer to my poor old mother," moans Pugnacious Pete. "I'll never see her sweet old face again."

In the midst of all this moaning and groaning, the cabin boy is the only person to do something sensible. He shins up one of the paltry palm trees and looks out to sea. Now he shouts, "Ship ahoy!" so loudly that the rest of the crew-members have to cover their ears. The rum has had an unpleasant effect on their eardrums.

But the cabin boy is right. Away on the horizon, a dark ship can just be seen in the gathering dusk.

"Set fire to something. Quick!" shouts Pete. The nearest large thing that would make a good blaze meets his eye and he advances towards it with menace.

A more sensible and sober sailor might have realized that it was not a good idea to set fire to the *Purple Pimple*, but Pete has never been sensible and is certainly not at this moment sober. Luckily, he is quite incapable of lighting a match or making a spark of any kind.

As night slips over the island, the imperilled pirates realize they have no hope of attracting the attention of the passing ship.

The next morning, with throbbing heads and pulsating eyeballs, the pirates spend some hours trying to persuade their brains to open their eyelids. It is therefore not until almost noon that they are able to look around and see that the mystery ship is sailing straight towards them.

"Hooray!" shouts Poisonous Pedro.

"Hooray!" shouts the cabin boy.

"Hooray!" shouts Pugnacious Pete.

"Help!" yell the sailors with one voice. They have spotted the approaching ship's dark sails, its black and white flag, its gleaming guns. It's a pirate ship and not just any old pirate ship. Blackhearted Bill, the nastiest navigator this side of the equator, sails in the *Burst Gumboil*. He is no friend to Pugnacious Pete.

Luckily for the crew of the *Purple Pimple*, Blackhearted Bill is as skilled a sailor as their own clueless captain. With a…

SchwAAAAck!

the *Burst Gumboil* sails smack into the *Purple Pimple* and bumps it off the island.

For five furious minutes, confusion reigns. As one crew sails through the air towards a sandy landing, the other crew jumps into the water and swims desperately after the drifting *Pimple*. The *Gumboil* is not drifting. It has become stuck in its turn, and Blackhearted Bill is berating his men as barnacle-bottomed blackguards.

Pugnacious Pete, who has always felt that a sailor's first duty is to stay *out* of the water, is not a great swimmer. Fortunately, his wooden leg floats beautifully and guides him back to his ship. Within a remarkably short time, considering the incompetence of all involved, the *Purple Pimple* is sailing towards the horizon.

Does Pete give a thought to the fate of Blackhearted Bill? Does the image of his dear old mother so much as cross his mind? Does the cabin boy get promotion and an extra ration of weevil-filled biscuit? If you don't know the answers to those questions by now, you haven't been paying attention. Take a deep breath and plunge straight into the next chapter.

Overboard!

Pugnacious Pete's favourite possession—
if you don't count his wooden leg—
is what he grandly refers to as the Sword
of Doom. This perfectly ordinary-looking
piece of pirate kit was, according to
Pete, wrenched from the grasp of
a Spanish prince moments
before Pete sent him to a
watery grave.

In fact, although it is true that the sword is of Spanish origin, Pete found it in a secondhand shop in the back streets of Cadiz. Nowadays, Pete has told the story of the proud but pathetic prince so often that he believes it himself. What is more, he is positive that the sword has Magical Powers.

Now Pete is as vile a villain as you are ever likely to meet. Just because he is too daft to do any real damage, it doesn't mean that he isn't bad through and through. He thinks nothing of doing a dozen dastardly deeds before breakfast. But Pete also has a silly and superstitious side. He really believes that while the Sword of Doom is in his possession, he will live to darken another day.

The incompetent crew of the *Purple Pimple* can't sail straight at the best of times. When the wind whips around the rigging with a vicious snarl and the sea boils evilly like the cook's so-called soup, this luckless bunch of puny pirates is a disgrace to the seven seas. The ship lurches from wave to wave, while the bosun cowers in an empty barrel, the cook comforts himself with cups of rum, and Pugnacious Pete himself is sick over the side without a thought of who or what is downwind.

At just this moment, as the *Purple Pimple* shudders under the shock of another slosh of sea over its gunwhales, our gallant (*hmmm*) captain cries out in alarm.

"Overboard!"

Up pops the bosun, hopeful that Pete himself may be wallowing in the waves. Up lurches the cook, bothered about the rum barrels. Up pops the cabin boy, hoping to be helpful. They find Pete pointing pitifully at the sea.

"The Sword of Doom!" he cries. "It's gone! Overboard! Give me your dagger, Bosun, you bucket of blubber! Quick!"

As the *Purple Pimple* sways like a blueberry blancmange, Pete starts hacking at the ship's side.

"Stop, Captain!" cries the cabin boy, leaping up. "Don't destroy the *Pimple* and everyone on her!"

Frankly, it would take some time to reduce a galleon the size of the *Purple Pimple* to kindling with only one dented dagger. Pete turns on the youngster with a blood-curdling bellow.

"Blithering bilge-rat! I'm not attacking the boat. I'm marking the spot where the Sword of Doom went over. When this storm stops, we'll know where to dive!"

"D-d-d-dive?" stammers the cabin boy, knowing only too well that Pugnacious Pete has no intention of putting his precious self in peril. "B-b-b-but…"

The boy's words are quite literally drowned by a massive wash of water that drenches the deck and everyone on it. When the crew-members rub the salt spray from their eyes, they find they are alone. There is no sign of Pugnacious Pete.

"Captain overboard!" shouts the bosun, clinging to the cook. "And I can't even mark the spot. He's taken my dagger to the deep!"

As the wind howls around them, the ill-fated followers of Pugnacious Pete lean over the side and stare into the stormy waters. Their emotions are, to be honest, mixed.

"It was my best dagger, too!" sniffs the bosun.

"No diving after all!" yells the cabin boy, failing to summon up a look of distress.

"A rum ration to shpare!" slurs the ship's cook.

Several other crew-members begin a hornpipe of celebration before they realize that dancing in a Force Nine Gale is not the brightest of ideas. (But then, if they'd been at all agile in the brainbox department, they wouldn't have sailed with Pugnacious Pete in the first place.)

It is at just this moment that a mighty wave, crashing onto the deck with pirate-pulverizing power, deposits a bedraggled buccaneer in their midst. It is Pugnacious Pete himself, drenched, dazed, but definitely alive.

"Don't just stand there!" yells Pete to his petrified crew. "Help me up!"

"Have you still got my dagger?" asks the bosun.

"You didn't find the Sword of Doom, did you?" asks the cabin boy, trying hard to look happy.

"I want to go home!" wails the cook, watching with horror as Pete downs a month's worth of his rum ration to steady his nerves.

Taking care of the captain fully occupies the crew for the next hour or so. It is not until Pete is once more in dry clothes and beginning to feel a little better that everyone notices the storm is over. The *Purple Pimple* is once again drifting gently across agreeably calm seas.

The moment the cabin boy has been dreading has arrived.

"Right," bellows Pete. "Here's a rope. Tie it round your middle, dive down and find the Sword of Doom. Here's the place." Pete points to an ugly notch in the woodwork.

"I'll float!" says the cabin boy, and knows, the moment he says it, that it's a mistake.

"I can soon fix that," growls Pete. He stuffs two cannon-balls into a stocking and ties it around the cabin boy's chest, giving him an extremely odd appearance.

Not surprisingly, the cabin boy is reluctant to leap overboard. Pugnacious Pete offers a friendly hand, or rather, a friendly boot.

Splosh! One small cabin boy and two large cannon-balls hit the water at the same time—and disappear from view with frightening speed.

"What do we do now?" asks the bosun.

"Now," says Pete, chillingly, "we wait."

"I shay," shays (sorry, says) the cook. "Shouldn't shomeone hold onto that rope?"

It's too late. As the crew watches, open-mouthed, the cabin boy's lifeline slips over the side and disappears under the water. For the second time that day, the crew of the *Purple Pimple* prepares to say farewell to one of its own. Too soon! With a triumphant shout, the cabin boy's head appears above the water. He is missing one lifeline and two cannon-balls, but against all the odds he triumphantly holds aloft … the Sword of Doom!

Pugnacious Pete, overcome by sentiment and rum, claps the cabin boy on the back. The lad is the hero of the hour. In what is perhaps the single most sensible move of his maritime career, the cabin boy decides to say nothing, nothing at all, about the wreck he found directly below the *Purple Pimple*. It contains the wares of one Juan Peseta, supplier of fancy goods to southern Spain (including certain back-street junk shops in Cadiz), who went down with his ship in a storm after unwisely overloading it with swords (of doom, definitely).

Becalmed!

Mariners moan (a lot) about bad weather. They have a horror of hurricanes. They have a terror of typhoons. I suppose it's understandable. Storms have a habit of upending the most valiant vessel and sending it to the deep. But there is something that pirates hate even more than rough seas—calm seas. Yes, there is nothing worse in a sailor's eyes than being stuck in the doldrums.

One afternoon a couple of weeks before Christmas, Captain Pugnacious Pete and his crew find themselves becalmed in the middle of a very Pacific Ocean. There is no land in sight. All that can be seen, stretching for mile upon nautical mile, is flat, sunny ocean. There are no waves. There is no wind. The sails are as slack as a pair of drawers on a washing line.

"Where are we, Bosun?" asks Pete, gazing at the chart and not at all sure which way up to hold it.

"Two hundred miles south of Barnacle Island, five hundred miles north of Gurgle Point and four hundred miles east of China," says the bosun, confident that Pete hasn't the faintest idea whether he is right or not.

"So what's this?" asks Pete, pointing to a purple patch on the map.

It is, in fact, an … er … *offering* from Poisonous Pedro after a meal of squid, but the bosun doesn't like to say so.

"It's called Revolting Reef," he grunts, glaring at Pedro. "Trust me. We don't want to go there."

"Are we on course?" asks Pete, suspiciously.

"Absolutely!" says the bosun, which, since he doesn't have the faintest idea where they are headed, is a miracle in itself.

"Then all we have to do is wait," says Pete reasonably. "Cabin Boy, bring me my banjo!"

Now, I believe I've mentioned the natural repugnance a sailor feels for windless weather. Even being becalmed, however, is a billion times better than listening to Pugnacious Pete on the banjo. He only knows one tune, which is something to do with someone being barmy, and he plays it over and over and over again. Very rapidly, it isn't only the person in the song who is barmy. Every member of the ship's company is crawling on the deck and calling for his mother.

Two hours of the banjo later, the crew decides to take desperate measures. They scoop up the glutinous remnants of yesterday's squid stew and stuff it into their ears. (It is, of course, silly to stuff *anything* into your ears *ever*, but you can understand it in the circumstances.)

Now squid stew is not fabulous food but it does have quite wonderful soundproofing qualities. For the rest of the afternoon, the crew-members are blissfully unaware of Pete's playing. They snooze in the sun and wait for the wind to get up.

But the wind, far from getting up, is having the longest lie-in of its life. The afternoon passes. The night passes. Two more long days crawl by. The squid stew smells so bad it has to be washed out of certain loathsome lugholes. Luckily, the sun has stretched the banjo strings. Although Pugnacious Pete is, in fact, playing "Al Barmy" for the three- thousand-and-forty-ninth time, it is no longer recognizable. In any case, even Pete is beginning to tire of it.

"There must be something we can do," he says. "Hasn't anyone got a pack of cards?"

There is silence. Pete himself ate the cards last time rations were running low.

"I've had an idea," says the cabin boy. "If there's no wind out there to fill the sails, why don't we make some wind ourselves?"

There is silence. Even the unwholesome crew of the *Purple Pimple* thinks this is a gross idea.

The cabin boy turns suddenly scarlet. "I didn't mean *that*!" he protests. "I was thinking, you know, of birthday cakes."

You don't often see a band of nautical ne'er-do-wells thinking of birthday cakes they have known and loved. The bosun sucks his thumb and clutches an imaginary teddy bear. It's the cook who gets the idea.

"You mean like blowing out the candles!" he says. "But will it work?"

"There's only one way to find out," replies Pete briskly. "Come on, all line up in front of the mainsail. Are you ready? Breathe in! One, two, three ... wait a minute, what are you doing on the sail, Pedro, you pathetic piece of poultry? You're making it twice the weight. Come back here and start flapping your wings or something. Now, are we ready? One..."

Pete is surprised to hear several thuds as members of the crew, purple and gasping, literally hit the deck. He has told them to breathe in but not, unfortunately, to breathe out.

Several minutes later, when oxygen levels are back to normal, a second attempt is made.

"Ready, steady, blow!" yells Pete.

None of the crew is at all familiar with Newton's Laws of Motion. In any case, their puny puffing makes no difference. The sail hangs limp. Pretty soon, the pirates are feeling limp, too. Birthday cake candles are one thing. Trying to summon up a Force Nine from a criminal crew close to collapse is something else. Everyone decides to take a rest.

It is at this point that Pete has a truly terrible idea. Terrible for everyone but him, that is. Thoughts of birthday cakes have reminded him of days gone by. And days gone by have brought to mind those Roman galleons powered by hundreds of sweating slaves, chained to their oars.

Pete looks around at his crew and feels depressed. Where are the rippling muscles required? Viewed in that light, the pirates look positively puny. Still, it's worth a try.

The try does not, in fact, last more than a couple of minutes. It soon becomes clear that there are no oars on board long enough to reach the water. The bosun's idea of cutting holes in the side of the ship near the waterline is universally shouted down. Sailors are quite rightly sensitive on the subject of holing their boats. "Water outside, sailors inside!" is their maxim.

Pete's plan to cut down the mast and make it into two giant oars also fails—but only because the saw on board is fit only for removing limbs or scraping barnacles from the bilge.

Then the ship's cook has a bright idea. "What we need," he says, "is an engine! Ships with engines don't need sails."

He is, of course, right. He is also almost two hundred years ahead of his time. If he can only cling to this thought instead of his rum bottle and the *Purple Pimple*, he will be a made man.

He can't, of course. "What?" cry the bosun and the cabin boy.

"Forget it," says the cook quickly. "I'm talking rubbish."

It may be the mention of rubbish, but the bosun decides to come out with some of his own.

"In my experience," he says pompously, "the wind always gets up when you don't want it to. When you're trying to have a picnic, for example. Or … or … climbing up the mast."

"That's right," says Pete. His eyes fall upon the hapless cabin boy. "Up!" he says. "And make it snappy."

It seems unfair that a boy starting at the bottom in nautical life should be asked to get to the top so rapidly. The cabin boy cowers. Pete reaches for his banjo. The cabin boy climbs. Up, up, up he goes, until…

All of a sudden, a fresh little breeze blows Pete's hat into the rigging and slaps into the sail with a hearty hello.

It's business as usual on the *Purple Pimple*. The sails flap and smack. The timbers creak and groan. Pugnacious Pete smacks. The bosun groans. The ship is speeding along once more, pitching and tossing as only a badly loaded, chronically crewed, atrociously trimmed vessel can.

Pete ponders over the map once more. Pedro adds a few more reefs to the region.

"South by southwest!" says Pete decisively, which just happens to be the way the ship is going anyway.

That night, as a stronger and stronger wind whistles around the *Purple Pimple*'s cabins, Pugnacious Pete and his crew sleep easier in their hammocks, lulled by the sway of the sea. Strangely, all have the same dream. In it, a tiny voice, from somewhere very high and far away, cries, "Help! Help! Help!" over and over again, in tones curiously like those of the cabin boy.

Marooned!

Pugnacious Pete, like most pirates, enjoys telling tall tales, drinking rough rum and musing on the daring and devilish deeds (mostly fictional) he has done. But Pete likes one thing more than any of the above— treasure! At the merest mention of doubloons, Pete goes weak at the knees.

Now there are two main ways for a pirate to get hold of the gleaming stuff. Both involve stealing, of course, but that doesn't matter to mariners with the morals of a shipworm. The first way is to find a big fat ship, laden to the gunwhales with gorgeous gold, and seize it by force. Considerable amounts of killing may be necessary. There is also a serious risk of being killed yourself. Big fat ships tend to have big fat forces on board.

Pete isn't keen on being killed. In fact, he isn't keen on anything that will put him at risk in any way. He has, in the past, been careless to say the least about his body parts (hence the wooden leg), and he dimly realizes that a pirate who loses more than one limb is likely to become an ex-pirate (not to mention an ex-person) pretty soon. So Pete has never vigorously pursued the seizing-ships option.

The other method of treasure retrieval is both easier and more difficult. It involves finding treasure that someone else has seized and hidden, usually on a desert island somewhere. You know the kind of thing—a parchment map and a cross marking the spot. There's often no killing involved and not much chance of getting a dagger in your own gizzard. BUT … laying your hands on a decent treasure map these days is not easy.

One blustery afternoon, when the ship's carpenter is bending Pete's ear about the serious state of the *Purple Pimple*'s timbers, an annoying yelling is heard above the slap of the sails and the groaning of the aforementioned timbers. Pete looks round for someone to punch, but there is no one else on deck except the bosun, who is asleep at the wheel.

It takes Pete several minutes to think of looking over the side, and when he does, he is not best pleased by what he sees.

Far below, bouncing on the choppy waves, is an unattractive-looking character in a small open boat. He has no oars and very little else in the way of luggage, food or water.
"Blooming barnacles!" cries Pete. "It's Treacherous Trevor!"

Pete and Trevor go back a long way in the pirating business. Indeed, they both once sailed on the *Adeline Acne*, an ill-fated vessel that met its doom largely because of the combined efforts of Pete and Trev to save it. However, more recent events, not unconnected with Pete's lack of limb, began a deadly emnity between the pirate pair. Pete and Trev have not exchanged a civil word for ten years.

Despite his perilous situation, Treacherous Trevor is not about to start now.

"Let me on board, you scummy excuse for a seaman!" shrieks Trevor.

"Not in a million years!" growls Pete. "And not tomorrow either!"

A look of low cunning comes over Trevor's foul face. "I've got something in-ter-est-ing here!" he chants in a singsong voice.

Pete is disgusted but he can't help himself. "What is it, wormbrain?" he charmingly enquires.

Then Treacherous Trevor waves what looks very much like … surely not! Yes, it is something resembling a treasure map!

Trevor's Treasure Map
P.T.O.

There follows one of those you-throw-it-up-first-no-take-me-on-board-first conversations that can go on and on. Frankly, life is too short to trouble ourselves with that. All you need to know is that four hours later (I told you they can go on and on), Pete and Trev are sitting down at the captain's table and peering at the map.

Neither of the two nefarious ne'er-do-wells wants to let anyone else in on the secret, so it takes them a terribly long time to locate the treasure island on Pete's sea charts. Even then, it's hard to be sure they have the right one. Luckily, it's not far away.

"Here's the plan," says Pete. "You and I will land on the island and find the treasure. Then we'll bring it back on board when it's dark and share it out. The rest of the crew need never know anything about it."

"Good idea," says Trevor sweetly.

If this polite exchange makes you suspicious, you're dead right.

That afternoon, Pugnacious Pete can be heard casually telling the bosun to anchor by a small, faintly familiar island and to break out the rum for the entire crew. The bosun can hardly believe his ears. But Pete's plan, for once, works like a dream. By the middle of the afternoon, no one is in any state to notice two greedy gold-seekers creeping down the gangplank and onto the shore.

"Which way now?" hisses Pete, for Treacherous Trevor has the map.

"This way!" squeals Trevor, plunging into the undergrowth. Within thirty seconds, Pete is alone, lost …
and livid.

Pugnacious Pete settles down under a palm tree by the shore. He tries hard not to think about treasure. He tries harder not to think about Treacherous Trevor. He tries hardest of all not to think about Treacherous Trevor creeping ever closer to some perfectly good treasure that should by rights (well, by wrongs) belong to only one person—Pugnacious Pete himself.

Pugnacious Pete doesn't find thinking easy. He finds not thinking even more difficult. Just when his brain has reached a degree or two below boiling point, it suddenly has another thing to worry about.

Boink!

Something very large and very hard hits Pugnacious Pete's heated headpiece.

Meanwhile, in a cave not a million miles away, Treacherous Trevor is puzzling over his treasure map. He feels sure that it will lead him to a chest positively overflowing with florins, drowning in doubloons, piled high with pieces of eight—if only he can work out which way up to hold it.

In the brains department, Treacherous Trevor is only slightly less challenged than Pugnacious Pete. He creeps out of the cave with a dim thought that he can find out which way is up by looking at the sun and his watch. It is a pity that he doesn't actually have a watch. He also hasn't considered that while he has been pondering over his parchment, night has fallen.

Suddenly, Trevor doesn't feel terribly happy about being in the dark on an unknown island. Without trying very hard at all, he can hear a horrible screeching from his left, a disturbing howling from his right, and a deeply worrying slithering sound from somewhere near his bare toes. Trevor—for the very first time in his life—begins to wish that Pugnacious Pete is by his side.

A second later, all thoughts of Pete fly out of Trevor's brain as he hears the grunting and screeching of a monstrous beast crashing through the undergrowth. It sounds like a dozen rhinos rushing to the attack. Whimpering, Trevor turns to flee back into his cave, but in the dark, he can no longer see it. Instead, he runs smack into a palm tree and clings to its trunk, making pathetic sounds and shivering like a jellyfish.

The beast is bellowing. It is thrashing through the trees. It is only inches away. It smells ghastly. It is … Pete!

As the moon struggles through the straggly clouds, Trevor and Pete recover
from the shock of their collision. In a surprisingly short time, Pete's pounding
and pudding-sharp mind is back on the business in hand.

"Did you find it?" he hisses.

"Find what?" asks Trevor, attempting
a casual whistle.

Pete takes him by the collar and demands
to see the map.

"The m-m-m-map?" asks Trevor, holding up his empty hands.
Clearly, the map has been dropped somewhere in the trampled undergrowth.
Equally clearly (or rather, equally unclearly), moonlight is inadequate lighting
for a fingertip search.

"There are lanterns on the *Pimple*," yells Pete. "Come on!"

But there is a problem in leaving a ship in the charge of a bosun too drunk to
notice if his captain is present. Sometimes, just sometimes, such a bosun might
take it into his head to set sail…

Swashbuckled!

Watching in disbelief as the *Purple Pimple* sails erratically away, even Treacherous Trevor and Pugnacious Pete, two seasoned sea-dogs, run out of salty language. The last oath dies away, and the full horror of the situation strikes both pirates. It is bad enough to be marooned on a small island alone. It is almost unbearable to be there in the presence of a truly obnoxious character—and as far as obnoxiousness goes, there isn't much to choose between Trev and Pete.

After spending a most uncomfortable night up a palm tree (for fear of wild animals below), Pete and Trev breakfast with little enthusiasm on coconuts and clams. The thought of this diet for weeks, months or … perish the thought … years adds another layer of gloom to an already overcast day.

Trawling about in his mind for something more cheerful to think about, Pete suddenly remembers the treasure … and the missing map. The same thought occurs at the same moment to his breakfast companion.

"Think I'll just go for a stroll," says Pete casually.

"Good idea. I'll come too," says Trevor, not deceived for a moment. But despite hours of aimless strolling in the general vicinity of the cave, no map can be seen. Pete and Trev sit down in shared despair.

"Maybe your crew will come back," says Trev, hopefully.

Pete snorts. He knows only too well the navigational ability of his men. The chance of them finding a small island in a very large ocean is tiny. Worse, they may not even want to! Pete regrets a number of cutting comments, peculiar punishments and weevil-infested meals he has doled out on the *Pimple* in the past.

Only two things keep the pirates together. One is Trevor's clam-opening penknife. The other is Pete's coconut-attracting head.

Whenever he sits down under a palm tree, a ripe coconut skitters across his skull. It saves a lot of climbing. A diet of clams and coconut is bad enough, but a diet of only clams or only coconuts is unthinkable. Somehow or other, the pirates manage not to strangle each other as the days pass.

Here's another point where we should skip forward a bit. I can tell you briefly that nothing at all exciting happens on the island for the best part of fourteen months. Beards and hair grow. The clam population decreases. That's it. We will fast-forward to a morning when the sky is blue, the sun is sparkling on

the dancing waves, and a set of white sails is seen on the horizon.
As soon as Pete spots the sails, he and his companion begin running up
and down the beach waving their arms. When this doesn't seem to have
any effect, they strip off their ragged clothes (avert your eyes if you need
to) and wave those instead. Clothed, these pirates are not wholesome.
Unclothed, they are a sight that any self-respecting ship would flee from.
Strangely enough, the unknown craft comes gradually closer.

As the galleon drops anchor in the bay, Treacherous Trevor and
Pugnacious Pete peer at it with increasing amazement. Its sails could
advertise washing powder. Their gleam is almost too much for Pete, who
is forced to swap his eyepatch to the other eye (he only wears it for
effect). Every timber of the ship is smooth and clean. There isn't a
barnacle or a trace of a passing seagull anywhere. On deck, sheets
(ropes to you and me) are neatly coiled. Some respectable washing
flies from the mast.

"You don't think…" Pete begins.

"It couldn't b-b-be!" stammers Trevor.

But it is. "Perfect Peregrine!" groan the
pongy pirates.

"Ahoy there, chaps!" comes a cheery voice, and
Perfect Perry wades ashore. As usual, he looks
impossibly handsome. His teeth glint as he smiles.
His cuffs are crisp. His curls are crisper.
His blue eyes positively twinkle.

"Been here long?" asks Perry,
looking with distaste at the
beards and hairstyles that
are fortunately hiding most of
the bodies in front of him.

"Not long," replies Pete carelessly. "Might stay on a bit, actually. Very pleasant climate. Very fine clams."

One of the most annoying things about Perfect Peregrine, apart from his mission to rid the sea of pirates, is that he is as clever as he is clean. He understands in a flash that there is more to the situation than meets the eye.

"So what brought you here?" he enquires genially. "Wildlife? Holiday? Treasure?"

Pete and Trev are hardened pirates. They are used to looking mean and deeply inscrutable. But frankly, after fourteen months, they are totally out of practice. At the mention of treasure, they twitch.

"Got a map?" asks Perfect Perry with a gleam in his eye. It is costly to keep a galleon as ship-shape as the trim *Maiden's Blush*.

"No," says Pete.

"Yes," says Trev, at the same moment. "I mean, no."

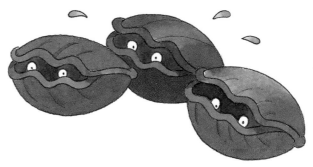

Perfect Perry never resorts to the types of torture with which Pugnacious Pete is familiar. The thumbscrews and the toetwisters are distasteful to him. But he makes up for a lack of ironware with more than his share of cunning.

"Fancy a bit of lamb stew?" he asks. "Cherry pie? Strawberry shortcake? Barrel of rum … purely medicinal, of course. Or maybe you'd rather carry on with the clams. Quite understand. Delicious shellfish."

He hasn't even finished speaking before Pete and Trev, visibly drooling, are clutching at his knees and begging to be taken on board the *Maiden's Blush.*

"All in good time, chaps," says Peregrine. "Let's have a little chat about maps first."

When Peregrine hears that the map has been lost, his smile and his charm both become a little chilly. Then he probes further.

"But you looked at the map pretty carefully?" he asks.

"Yes, but we don't remember," says Pete gruffly.

Perfect Perry appears cheered by this news. "Of course you don't," he replies soothingly. "Now come on board and have … well, a bath would be a good start, I think."

That evening, blissfully full of lamb stew and strawberry shortcake, and cleaner than he has been since his mother last excavated his ears, Pete swings gently in a hammock while the ship's boy plays soulful ditties on the mandolin. Pete wonders whether to jump up and ask if there's a banjo on board, but he decides against it. And, just as he begins to feel sleepy, he hears a somewhat familiar voice in his ear.

"You are beginning to feel sleepy," it says with uncanny accuracy. "You are beginning to feel very, very sleepy."

Pete closes his eyes. The voice drones on.

"You are fast asleep. You are thinking back to the last treasure map you examined. You are seeing it in your mind's eye. You are taking this pencil and copying it onto this paper. You are drawing very carefully and not going over the edge. You are not even thinking about chewing the very fine pencil. You are finishing your drawing. You are handing it over … and the very fine pencil. You are sitting up in your sleep. You are walking across the deck. How beautiful the water looks. How inviting. What a lovely moment for a swim…"

It is the squawking of Poisonous Pedro that brings Pete to his senses. It is the digging of Poisonous Pedro's claws into Perfect Peregrine's scalp that causes the howling. It is the sight of Perfect Peregrine's pristine hairpiece gliding through the air that persuades his crew to join with Pete and Treacherous Trevor in a most satisfying mutiny.

After all, clean living and deck-swabbing can only hold a crew's interest for so long. After a while, any self-respecting seaman wants to give up baths and swear a bit. As Perfect Peregrine performs a perfect breaststroke towards the island so recently home to Trev and Pete, the crew gives a hearty cheer for its new captains and sets sail for the Spanish Main, while Poisonous Pedro sets about giving the spotless sails a little more of a lived-in look.

Suckered!

It is remarkable how quickly standards on a well-ordered ship can sink. Within hours of the arrival of Pugnacious Pete and Treacherous Trevor, there are weevils in the biscuits and the lamb stew has acquired that strange, slimy consistency so familiar from the *Purple Pimple*.

To Pete and Trev it feels like home, although Pete does still think fondly of his old *Pimple* and wonders what wide ocean she is sailing now. He also has plans of deep and dark revenge against the bosun, should he ever come across that scurvy seaman again.

There are, of course, things about the *Maiden's Blush* (or the *Maiden's Rash* as she soon comes to be known) that Pete finds strange. For a start, he has a helmsman who can read a chart. For the first time in his life, Pete has half an idea of where he is going. He's not sure he likes this. It takes the sense of adventure out of pirating somehow.

Secondly, Pete has a co-captain. He is absolutely certain he doesn't like that! In fact, Treacherous Trevor is becoming more annoying every day—and more treacherous, too. It's not long before both captains spend all their time plotting against each other. It is only because they are quite hopeless at planning that both are still on board.

At night, the captains sleep in hammocks in the captain's cabin. Pete has been careful to position himself over a particularly creaky floorboard, so that he has warning if anyone happens to come creeping up. He is also, in case the worst comes to the worst, near a Pete-sized hatch. A dip in the ocean is better than a dagger in the ribs, he thinks.

One dark, sultry night, Pete and Trevor are swaying gently in their hammocks. As usual, each has one eye open, although Pete has chosen to open the eye under his eyepatch, which makes him believe the night is particularly dark.

When Pete feels something clammy curling its way around his neck, his first thought is that Trevor is up to his old tricks.

"Oh no, you don't!" he cries, and sinks his teeth into Trevor's arm. He can't help noticing two significant things. Trev doesn't shout out.
His arm is strangely rubbery.

Then a second arm wraps itself with astonishing strength around Pete's knees. Pete is beginning to panic when a third arm begins to squeeze him around his rather large middle.

Now even Pete, not famous for his thinking skills, knows that Treacherous Trevor only has two arms.

As Pete writhes in the grip of his assailant, his eyepatch falls off. A shaft of moonlight shines through the cabin. On the other side, Treacherous Trevor's eyes are bulging as one massive suckered arm squeezes his face. Three suspiciously similar suckered arms are hugging Pete in a far from affectionate way.

Suddenly, the *Maiden's Rash* seems to leap in the water. Pete, deposited rather quickly on his head on the floor, doesn't notice for a moment that the deadly grip has ceased. He is more aware of the fact that Trev's toe is wedged up his (Pete's) nose.

A few minutes of confusion, cursing and toe-removal follow, during which the *Maiden's Rash* is violently shaken (actually, this helps with the toe-removal). When Pete and Trev at last scramble out on deck, the sight that meets their eyes as dawn glimmers on the horizon is gruesome indeed.

The ship is in the grip of a squid so huge that it is waving the *Maiden's Rash* about like a toy. Pete can hear the crew rattling about below. Clinging on for dear life, he and Trev have an urgent council of war.

"I suggest we hack off its arms," says Pete, clutching the Sword of Doom.

"There are dozens of them!" gasps Trevor. Counting is not his strong point. "There are harpoons in the hold."

Pete hasn't the faintest idea how to throw a harpoon. It sounds dangerous and difficult. Besides, he is beginning to think there is a fatal flaw in all these plans.

"We might just make it cross," he yells. "Well, crosser. What if it decides to dive? Maybe we should try being nice to it!"

Neither of the pirates has any idea of how to set about being nice to a squid. Finally, Trev has a thought and heads for the galley. Surely a well-fed squid is a happy squid?

Working on the same lines, Pete looks around for his old banjo. Soothing music, he thinks, might calm the beast. Of course, Pete's banjo is still on board the *Purple Pimple*, but there is a mandolin.

Pete lashes himself to the mast so that he has two hands free. Trev, meanwhile, is filling the cannon with leftover lamb stew (now several weeks old) and preparing to fire in the general direction of what he takes to be the squid's mouth.

Pete's banjo playing is poor. His efforts on the mandolin are worse. Within two seconds, the unsuspecting squid is assailed by Pete's version of "What Shall We Do With the Drunken Sailor?" (played at half speed in the wrong key) and a faceful of smelly stew. It does not hesitate. The *Maiden's Rash* is dumped unceremoniously back in the water, and the squid heads at top speed for the peace of the deep.

"I knew my playing would work," says Pete, struggling to free himself from the mast.

"What do you mean? It was me feeding it that did it!" shouts Trev. "That's typical of you…"

And so, to the happy sound of captains complaining, the *Maiden's Rash* sails on towards adventures new.

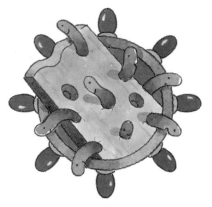

Timber!

The oceans of the world are wide. They are, in fact, twice as wide as the lands of the world, on which millions of human beings trudge up and down daily. By comparison, the traffic on the wide, blue, wet stuff is tiny. It should be well nigh impossible for two vessels with a vast ocean between them to collide. You can guess what is coming…

Late one night, when Pete and Trev are, as usual, hovering delicately between sleep and suspicion, a skull-shattering shock hurls them both from their hammocks. This time, it is Pete's bottom that bears the brunt of the impact, while Trev ricochets around the walls before coming to rest in the hammock he has recently left.

Pete's first confused thought is of squid. You will understand why. His second is that Treacherous Trevor is up to his old tricks. He doesn't get as far as a third thought because it is at this moment that the painfulness of his posterior truly strikes him.

"Owwwww!" yells Pete.

"Whaafnaafnum?" demands Trevor, his voice muffled by the hammock, which has spun around and made him into a kind of sea-going sausage.

"H-e-l-p!" comes a pitiful voice from far below, followed by other pitiful voices sending much the same message.

Pete staggers on deck and peers through the gloom. There is something strangely familiar about the shouting and splashing surrounding the ship.

Just then, a beam of moonlight struggles through the ragged clouds. Pete gasps. He thinks of his bruised bottom and gasps again. But really, his first gasp was the most important one. All around, the sea looks like soup. That is, it looks like watery stuff with bits floating in it—which is what soup is, really.

On closer inspection, there appear to be two kinds of bits. Most are bits of wood. In fact, bits of wood that look suspiciously as if they have once been bits of ship. Pete looks around in alarm, but there are no disturbing glugging sounds coming from the *Maiden's Rash*. She has all her important parts and does not seem to be about to sink into the said soup.

The other floating bits also resemble chunks of wood but are, in fact, people. And not just any people. These are very familiar people indeed.

"Captain!" yells one of them. "Captain, my dear old darling! Come and have a swim. It's lovely once you're in!"

"Bosun!" Pugnacious Pete can hardly believe his eyes. There is his errant second-in-command, apparently as much under the influence as ever. But if that is the bosun, where is the *Purple Pimple*?

Suddenly, Pete's heart seems as bruised as his bottom. Even pirates have feelings. All around him, scattered on the waves, are the remains of his favourite flagship. The *Pimple* is no more.

Much later, as the sun rises over the *Maiden's Rash*, Pete's sadness turns, predictably enough, to fury. The crew of the *Purple Pimple* is dripping dismally on the deck. Only the bosun, for obvious reasons, is still resolutely cheerful.

"What have you done to my ship, you blithering blister on a barnacle?" yells Pete, gesturing wildly at the waves, where pathetic remnants of the aforementioned vessel are still bobbing bravely.

"We were run into," says the bosun, speaking very distinctly but not very tactfully, "by a big fat tub called the … er … the *Measle*, or something like that."

"You were not run into, herring head!" shouts Pete. "*We* were run into! Why couldn't you look where you were going? You've destroyed a perfectly … perfectly … fine friend…" There is a catch in Pete's pugnacious voice.

"It wasn't perfectly fine, you know." The ship's carpenter decides to add a word. "Those worms were past dealing with. The tiniest tap could have burst the *Pimple*. I often told the bosun so."

"And we were sailing under desperate difficulties," the bosun goes on blithely, "after you jumped ship, Captain…"

"Jumped ship!" Pugnacious Pete becomes purple with rage. "I did not jump ship! I merely … er … went ashore for a bit. When I came back, you were gone! Jumped ship, indeed! The only person doing any jumping here, you whelk-brained sea slug, will be you. Walking the plank always seemed a silly idea to me, when a swift swish with the Sword of Doom could do the job, but it's beginning to look attractive. At noon today, Bosun, you'll be taking

your final constitutional."

As the sun continues to climb the sky, and the effects of the night before begin to wear off, the bosun starts to understand the seriousness of his situation. He cudgels his brains for a way to get around his old captain.

He might have succeeded, too, if it hadn't been for Treacherous Trevor. When finally released from his hammock, Trev is peevish to say the least. He has missed all the fun of the rescues. He has missed seeing Pete turn purple. The only bit of fun remaining, as far as he can see, is the prospect of the bosun walking the plank.

Pete, of course, is anxious not to look soft in front of Trev. So when the bosun returns first Pete's favourite eyepatch and then Pete's beloved banjo, the co-captain hardens his heart against his erstwhile number two.

"It's time," he says at last. "Now, who's got the plank?"

There is no suitable plank on board the *Maiden's Rash*, so the crew fish a suitable bit of the *Purple Pimple* out of the sea and set it up on deck, nailing it down at one end but letting it wobble dangerously at the other, where it overhangs the sea.

The carpenter from the *Purple Pimple* seems strangely excited by all this. At least, he keeps jumping up and down and trying to attract Pete's attention. Pete ignores him.

"Come here, scum bucket," he invites the bosun, with his usual irresistible charm.

The bosun tries humour. He tries pleading. He tries getting down on his knees and weeping. Pete is not impressed. Waving the Sword of Doom carelessly near to the bosun's nose, Pete urges the sobbing seaman onto the plank.

"Now, walk, you sliver of squid slime!" yells Pete.

The bosun tries. He really does. But his knobbly knees are knocking together so ferociously that he can barely put one foot in front of the other. When he reaches the middle of the plank, he stops.

Pete has had enough. With a roar, he charges onto the plank, swiping wildly with the Sword of Doom. Taunting and tickling with its tip, he urges the bosun towards the very end of the plank.

The plank sways. The bosun totters. Pete, holding out the famous blade, is better balanced, but even he turns a little green around the gills. Back on deck, the ship's carpenter begins to make little squeaking noises.

And then... Craa-a-aaa-aaa-eeee-a-aaaak!

The plank snaps in half and into the sulky sea tumble the bosun, Pugnacious Pete and several hundred ship worms who were wiggling their way out of the plank.

"I tried to tell him," cries the ship's carpenter, running to the side.

Far below, Pugnacious Pete is clinging to the wreckage of the *Purple Pimple*, while swiping at the bosun, who is clutching another piece nearby. Pete would be safer if he let go of the Sword of Doom, but he remembers the last time he lost the wondrous weapon in the deep and holds onto it with grim determination.

"Do something!" yells Pete to the watchers high above on the *Maiden's Rash*. They do. They laugh.

Treacherous Trevor finds that he has not, after all, missed the chance to see Pete at his most purple.But the bosun realizes that his chance has come to redeem himself. Carefully avoiding the swinging Sword of Doom, he drags Pugnacious Pete to the side of the ship, where the cabin boy has thoughtfully let down a ladder.

Later that night, as he looks around at so many familiar faces, Pete reflects that the *Maiden's Rash* is looking and feeling more and more like the much-lamented *Purple Pimple*.

And, far below, several worms from the *Pimple* begin the happy task of chomping their way through the trusty timbers of the *Maiden*. It's an ill wind...

Scuppered!

Life on the ocean wave is rarely comfortable and frequently dangerous. Pugnacious Pete has always, so to speak, sailed pretty close to the wind, but recently even he has begun to think that things are a little *too* exciting on board the *Maiden's Rash*. Even if you don't count psychopathic squid and mid-ocean collisions, there is the perennial problem of Treacherous Trevor.

For Trevor certainly is treacherous—and not in a nice way. In recent weeks, Pete has found Dutch Death Fish in his spare underpants, broken glass in his boots, and Cantonese Killer Crabs in his hammock. He has also seen Trev muttering with various members of the combined crew of the *Rash* and the *Pimple*. The word "mutiny" strolls in a sinister way through the darkest corners of Pete's mind.

As Pete becomes increasingly ill at ease, the crew, too, gets edgier. Soon, everyone is creeping around, constantly looking over their shoulders and jumping at the creak of a plank or the squawk of a parrot. Of course, they are bumping into each other a lot, too. (It's the looking over the shoulder that does it. You really need wing mirrors if you are going to go in for a lot of that sort of thing.)

One afternoon, when dark storm clouds are billowing above the *Maiden's Rash,* and a deep sense of foreboding is swirling around the topsail, a ship is sighted on the horizon.

"A sail! A sail!" cries the cabin boy, wriggling in the rigging.

"Aha!" cries Pete, leaping to his feet. He has been sitting on the deck, a pistol in one hand and the Sword of Doom in the other, wishing he had a better idea of Treacherous Trevor's precise whereabouts at that moment.

Now, the possibility of some action at last—against an unknown enemy instead of an only-too-familiar one—stirs Pete's blood. Who knows what may be on the fast-approaching ship? Gold? Jewels? Chocolate biscuits? Pete lets out a bloodthirsty yell.

"Yo ho ho! What manner of ship is she?" he asks the cabin boy.

Thwack! The luckless cabin boy lands suddenly at Pete's feet. Well, foot. His face is white. His lips are trembling. His fingers are quivering. And not all of this is due to the fact that he has landed on one of the Cantonese Killer Crabs.

"What is it, boy?" yells Pete, impatient for news.

The cabin boy twitches. "It's D-D-D-D-D...!" he tries.

"Dutch? Danish? Drifting? Dusty?
Loaded with Digestives?" asks Pete.

"No! It's D-D-D-D-D...!" There is a look of
agony on the cabin boy's face. (The Killer
Crab isn't looking too healthy either.)

Pete's brow clears. Of course, it's another pirate ship.
"Oh, it's Desperate Derek?"

"No! D-D-D-D-D...!"

Other crew members join in the game. "Dark-hearted Dave? Dire Dominic?
Dastardly Donald?"

As the cabin boy struggles to reply, the strange ship has been gaining on the
Maiden's Rash. It's as evil a craft as you will ever see. As Pete, Trev and their
crew look up at last, the awful truth dawns on them. It is much, much
worse than Dark-hearted Dave, Dire Dominic, or Dastardly Donald.
With one voice, they gasp...

"Dreadful Doris!" and they turn to look at Pugnacious Pete, who is making a desperate attempt to throw himself overboard.

"Oh no, you don't!" says Treacherous Trevor, grabbing his co-captain without ceremony. "This I have to see!"

Quaking, Pugnacious Pete is dragged across the deck. At the same moment, the captain of the approaching ship, named, as is now clear, the *Athlete's Itch*, leaps lithely on board the *Rash*. It is Dreadful Doris herself, the meanest, baddest, fiercest pirate the world has ever known.

"Hello, Pete, you miserable maggot," she cries, in a voice that could stop a tornado in its tracks.

"Hello, Mum," mutters Pete.

There are words that are rarely said and even more rarely written, but I am going to write them now… *poor old Pete*. He may be bad. He may be ugly. He may be unhygienic. But no one deserves a mother like Dreadful Doris. She has a voice like a foghorn. She lives to harass and humiliate. She dresses in a way that would make any son shudder. She has terrible taste in earrings. And she is completely unaware of any of these failings.

Pete looks with panic at his crew. To a man, they turn away and begin whistling. There is no choice. Pete stumbles forward to be embraced by the woman whose perfume is the only known cure for an infestation of ship worms.

Poor old Pete. He sits on the deck with his mother, while she reminisces in a voice that reaches the top of the topsail and the bottom of the bilge. She leaves nothing out. Pete's potty training. Pete's lack of success with girls. Pete's personal hygiene problems.

Pete is well and truly scuppered.

And now, Doris declares, she will invite the crew of the *Maiden's Rash* to a special supper on board the *Athlete's Itch*—that is if Pete's sensitive stomach is up to it.

Pete shuts his eyes and prays for the arrival of a giant squid.

That night, on board the *Athlete's Itch*, Pete endures tortures that are too painful for me to mention. Suffice it to say that the evening begins with Dreadful Doris showing Pete's baby pictures and gets worse. Poor Pete can't even drown his sorrows in rum, for the eagle eye of his mother glitters alarmingly if he so much as toys with a tankard.

Of course, everyone else enjoys the evening enormously, and none more so than Treacherous Trevor. Nothing in the world delights him so much as to see Pugnacious Pete in agony. Dutch Death Fish and Cantonese Killer Crabs cannot do half the damage of a mother in full flood.

It is very late when an all-too-sober Pete staggers to his hammock at last. He doesn't even bother to check it for broken glass or sea snakes. Blessed oblivion, by whatever means, is all that he can hope for.

For three ghastly days, Pete endures the presence of his mother. Eventually, he enters a weird world of his own, where he tries to blot out the horror of what is happening around him. And that is, perhaps, why he really has no idea of something that is happening right under his nose.

Others notice a softening in Dreadful Doris. Ship worms shudder to find that she is wearing more perfume than usual. A new tattoo appears on her brawny forearm. She wears her hat at a jaunty angle and her earrings become slightly less dangerous. And she takes to singing as she strolls.

It's not a pleasant sound by any means, and the Killer Crabs all scuttle back to Canton as soon as she starts, but it is an improvement on the paint-stripping powers of her usual voice.

Pete, however, notices none of this. You can imagine the shock, then, when he enters the captains' cabin on the *Maiden's Rash* one day to find Dreadful Doris, his mother and tormentor, locked in a passionate embrace with Treacherous Trevor!

"Darling Petey-poops," yells Doris with a bashful smirk, "Trevor and I are going to tie the knot. Meet your new daddy!"

Pete's mind is unable to grasp this fresh awfulness. Does this mean…? Will Trev and Doris live happily ever after *here on the Maiden's Rash?*

But Doris is still speaking. "I'm sorry, sweetie. Trev and I will be sailing off tomorrow on our honeymoon. Can you manage without your dear old mum?"

A joyous fact is bubbling up from Pete's boots and making its way to his brain. Doris is leaving. Trev is leaving. Together. For ever. Today!

For the first time in weeks, Pugnacious Pete smiles. "I'll try," he says.

Torched!

Huddled on the windward side of Sir Bertilak Odorous's castle was something even meaner and more miserable than the noisome knight. It was a village called Dump. And yes, it really was a dump. When Sir Bertilak's ancestors first built a small fort on the mound on the valley floor, they simply threw their rubbish over the battlements. After a few years, they had to wade through deer bones and discarded dishcloths every time they went in or out of the fort, so Tlac the Terrible (Sir Bertilak's great-great-great-great-great-great grandfather) decreed that in future rubbish should only be thrown in one direction.

Now, in medieval times (and still, some would say, today), where there's rubbish, there's a living to be made. It wasn't long before the growing dump below the growing castle became a scurvy scavenging-ground. Various unwholesome characters scurried about there day and night —and I'm not talking about the rats.

You might think that deer bones and discarded dishcloths would be of little use to anyone, but you'd be amazed (and probably appalled) by what can be done with them. One or two of the scurriers became rich enough to wear shoes. Then, one day, an eagle-eyed boy spotted something twinkling in the remains of a pig pie. In throwing the offending dish over his shoulder, the current lord had thrown a large gold and ruby ring at the same time. Its finder couldn't believe his luck.

Finders of gold and ruby rings often fondly believe that their new-found wealth can be kept a secret. It can't. Frankly, swanning around in a new set of rags is a bit of a give-away. Pretty soon, there were even more scurriers on the dump, as more and more young hopefuls came to try to make their fortunes.

It wasn't long before the traffic between the castle and the dump was squirming in both directions. The vile village was soon supplying the castle with everything from kitchen knaves to kitchen knives. Some historians even believe that it supplied the family name, as well. Nothing, after all, could be more odorous than Dump.

Which, now that you have had a brief history of that sorry collection of hovels, brings us back to the story. Sir Bertilak, not one to learn from experience, still harbours ambitions to be a great dragon-slayer. The problem, as I have hinted before, is that dragons are unpredictable and unco-operative creatures. They have, on the whole, more sense than to wander about on mountain passes crying, "Slay me! Slay me!"

Sir Bertilak hadn't actually seen a dragon in the last seventeen years, but it is hard to acquire a reputation for dragon-slaying in a dragon-drought. His habit, in times of crisis, was always to consult an expert. They may give useful information. At the very least, they are someone else to blame when things go wrong. When there is a lack of dragons, however, there tends to be a lack of dragon experts. Sir Bertilak was forced to fall back on an exceedingly ancient tome entitled: *Ye Booke of Dragones: all ye ever sought to know.*

Sir Bertilak was not a great reader. He settled down with a dozen capons and a hogshead of ale and threw the book at his page, Porrit. When Porrit had picked himself up out of the evil-smelling rushes on the floor, he began to read.

The book was a large one. For the next three days, Porrit read steadily on while Sir Bertilak, munched, quaffed, burped, snored and rumbled in the corner. By Wednesday evening, Porrit had gone through "Dragon Biology", "The Life-cycle of the Dragon", "Dragon Habitats", and "Dragon Migration: Fact or Fiction?" It wasn't until he came to "Hunting Dragons" that Sir Bertilak woke up and took notice.

Like many manuals of its day, *Ye Booke of Dragones* went into great detail about how to track the beasts in question. Both Porrit and his master learnt more about dragon droppings than they had ever wished to know. The method for finding out if a dropping was fresh was particularly disgusting and put Sir Bertilak off his haunch of venison for several minutes.

"Signs of Singing," read Porrit, moving swiftly on.

"Singing? Dragons don't sing!" bellowed Sir B.

"Sorry, sire," Porrit looked ahead. "I read it wrong. They don't sing. They singe."

The knight began to look interested. A couple of weeks earlier, one of the thatched hovels of Dump had gone up in flames. At the time, a cooking fire with one too many logs on it had been blamed, but suddenly Sir Bertilak wasn't so sure. What if a passing dragon had been the culprit? It was well known that dragons, especially in the summertime, could be careless with their breathing.

Sir Bertilak couldn't be bothered to listen to the rest of the book. He felt he was on to something. As usual when the loathsome lord had a bee in his bonnet, he didn't keep quiet about it. He sent out guards to every part of his lands asking for details of any recent fire, however small.

It was a fatal mistake. No one wanted to say they had nothing to report. The guards were large, loutish and armed. In settlements that had not had a fire for centuries, enterprising inhabitants made sure that a few flickering flames were soon (only slightly) out of control somewhere in the village.

Naturally, in some places the fires escaped from management and burned down a few homes in the process, but that can seem a small price to pay when a guard is parting your hair with his halberd.

Ever wishing to placate their lord and master, the foul folk of Dump set more fires than anyone else.

After a night on which half the hovels in Dump burned down, Sir Bertilak was in a fever of excitement.

"There's been no report of this level of dragon activity for centuries," he crowed. "And it's getting closer all the time. Tonight, Porrit, we'll lie in wait. Tomorrow, there'll be a scaly skin hanging from my battlements."

A man like Sir Bertilak doesn't suffer discomfort lightly. All that day, his minions rushed about setting up a luxurious camp right next to Dump. In fact, they set it up twice. The first time, with the wind in the wrong direction, evidence of the presence of Dump was all too strong. Even Sir Bertilak, not renowned for being fragrant, felt it was too much. The camp was rebuilt on the other side of Dump.

That night, after a good supper and with a hand-picked team around him just in case, Sir Bertilak ordered the lights in the camp to be doused. In darkness, he waited for the arrival of as many dragons as might decide to call.

Hours passed. The moon rose. But no snuffling, snorting or flapping of dragon wings disturbed the night. Sir Bertilak and his men had dozed off over their shields when a jaw-juddering shout went up.

Fire!

A youngster from Dump, unaware that the fire-setting system had been suspended, had thrown an enthusiastic torch out of a window—right into the dragon-hunters' camp.

Next morning, looking slightly silly without his eyebrows, Sir Bertilak Odorous planned his next campaign. There was no doubt in his mind that a dastardly dragon had very nearly ambushed him the night before. The dragon must be dealt with.

He needed another plan…

Scorched!

A suit of armour is a wonderful thing if someone with less than friendly intentions is launching spears, rocks or rotten eggs in your direction. Most of the time, such menacing missiles simply bounce off—and if you're lucky, they bounce right back and clonk the person who threw them.

But if you wear armour when a dragon is showing an irritating interest, you are likely to feel as if you are sitting in a saucepan—and someone has turned the gas on. You start by feeling pleasantly warm, then unpleasantly warm, then horribly hot, then steam starts to come out of your poleyns—not a pretty sight.

Sir Bertilak Odorous, who had the misfortune to discover the fricasséed remains of his (admittedly unpleasant) uncle outside a dragon's cave in the Murky Mountains, was determined that such a fate would never befall *him*. He took himself off to the most famous inventor in the kingdom to commission an air-conditioned costume that would keep out lances, swords and other unsettling spikes but also be fire- and flame-proof.

Admittedly, the result looked odd. It wasn't easy to move in it, either, but that's a hazard of most suits of armour. Watching a knight in battle is like seeing a slow-motion action replay. Sir Bertilak decided that the suit must be tested before he would wear it. He looked about for a miserable menial who wouldn't make a fuss if slightly singed. His eye at once fell upon his unfortunate page, Porrit.

Now Porrit was poor, underfed and badly dressed, but he wasn't stupid. He knew perfectly well that dragon-proof-suit testing came high on the Most Dangerous Careers list. He pointed out in a most polite way that a suit built for a large and manly knight would not fit a little and boyish page.

Sir Bertilak snorted. The words "lily-livered pond scum" and "knock-kneed noodle" were some of the kinder ones he used. In short, he told Porrit that if he didn't climb into the suit straight away, he would be shoved in head first and have to make the most of it.

So it was that later that day an unhappy Porrit found himself sitting forlornly on a rock somewhere in the middle of the Murky Mountains. He was, of course, also in the middle of the dragon-proof armour. He was too short to see out of the visor and none of the bendy parts of the suit coincided with his own bendy parts, so moving was out of the question. All he could do was sit on his rock and wait for the worst. Namely, a dragon.

Now, it's a funny thing about dragons. You wait for years and years—sometimes for centuries and centuries—for one and never see the twitching of a scaly tail. Then three come along all at once.

That afternoon, it felt to Porrit as if the minutes were crawling past. It felt as if several other little things were crawling about inside his suit, too, but it's very hard to itch yourself in over-sized armour. Pretty soon, Porrit was in agony.

The page didn't know what to do with himself. It felt as if every part of him itched, from his little toe to the top of his ears. He tried squiggling and wriggling around inside his suit. In the process, he fell right off his rock and found himself lying on his back like an overturned tortoise.

There was no way he could right himself.

It was at this precise moment that the aforementioned three dragons came sauntering along the mountain track. Porrit couldn't see them, but he could hear a lot of scuffling and grunting, and something that sounded suspiciously like sniggering.

Yes, it was sniggering. The dragons looked at the object on the path and simply couldn't help giggling. Why human beings wanted to put themselves inside oddly-shaped tin cans had always been a mystery to them. This one, however, looked odder than most.

A lesser animal would have been suspicious—perhaps even frightened. But dragons had long ago realised that they had nothing to fear from humans. It was fun to taunt them now and again. The miserable little creatures had nasty wet noses and couldn't breathe fire to save their lives. You had to feel sorry for them, really.

The dragons' giggles subsided. They stood on the path in the sunshine looking at the object by their toes. Porrit, hearing only silence outside, kept very still. He waited. The dragons waited.

Thwummp!

One of the dragons stopped waiting and leapt into action. He wondered what the strange shiny thing with the human in it would look like rolling down a mountainside.

From the dragons' point of view, it was marvellous. The suit of armour bounced from rock to rock, making a satisfying clanging sound with every impact.

From Porrit's point of view, it was probably the single most uncomfortable thing that had ever happened to him. And when you consider that he had worked for Sir Bertilak Odorous for five years, that's saying quite a lot.

Oomph! Porrit's head hit the inside of his helmet. *Thwack!* His knee bashed an outlet pipe. *Thud!* two bendy bits of armour bent—but Porrit didn't.

A dauntingly dented suit of armour ricocheted down the mountain and into the valley below. It ended up, as luck would have it, at the foot of the mound on which Sir Bertilak's castle brooded. The   battered article was carried into the castle and dropped without ceremony in the middle of the courtyard.

Both Sir Bertilak and the famous inventor peered down at it.

"Disappointing," murmured the inventor.

"Disastrous," growled Sir Bertilak.

No one gave a thought to the unfortunate inhabitant of the armour. It was only when he heard some wheezing sounds and a vague moaning that it occurred to the nasty knight to order the armour to be opened.

Many of the bystanders averted their eyes as the helmet of the suit was prised off. They were very much afraid that Porrit would emerge in more pieces than he went in.

Luckily, the page who was fished out of the mangled metal was still recognizably Porrit. He wouldn't have won any beauty contests and he was a little shaky on his legs, but all the essential bits were still present.

"Well?" demanded Sir Bertilak. "Did you meet any dragons, boy? Does the suit work?"

Porrit paused. He decided to start with the good news. "It is," he said, "fire-proof, flame-proof, singe-proof and scorch-proof...."

"I knew it!" squealed the inventor.

Toasted!

Sir Bertilak pondered his dragon problem for some time. His forebears had also had a dragon problem, but theirs was a case of too many dragons, not too few. The ne'er-do-well knight needed to summon up at least one fire-breathing creature if his reputation as a dragon-slayer were to survive.

    As Sir Bertilak fulminated in his
castle, clouds gathered overhead,
servants scuttled about, superstitious
and scared, while thunder roared (and Sir Bertilak
roared, too) and lightning flashed (and Sir Bertilak
hurled unsuspecting minions from the windows). Trapped
inside, the noisome knight had no choice but to brood upon
his lack of performance in the death-to-dragons field. The only
good thing about the storm was that all the smouldering fires in the
countryside sizzled out. The bad thing was that all those left homeless
by recent conflagration got very wet indeed.

The more he pondered, the more it seemed to Sir Bertilak that an expedition, uncomfortable and costly as this would be, was essential. Everyone knew that dragons lived in the Murky Mountains. Plumes of smoke could be seen coming from the highest peak from time to time, which was a sure sign. Instead of waiting for dragons to come to him, Sir Bertilak decided to go out and confront the risky reptiles in their lairs.

Naturally, young Porrit, the hapless page, was to be of the party. For one thing, he was the only person in the land who could read a map. Although the maps of the area were vague in the extreme, there was a very ancient one with exciting annotations. "Here be dragones," it said, in the middle of some pointy things meant to represent the Murky Mountains. It also said, "Here be man-eating frogs," near the Damp Swamp and "Here be headless giants," near the town of Gluggle, renowned for its ale shops.

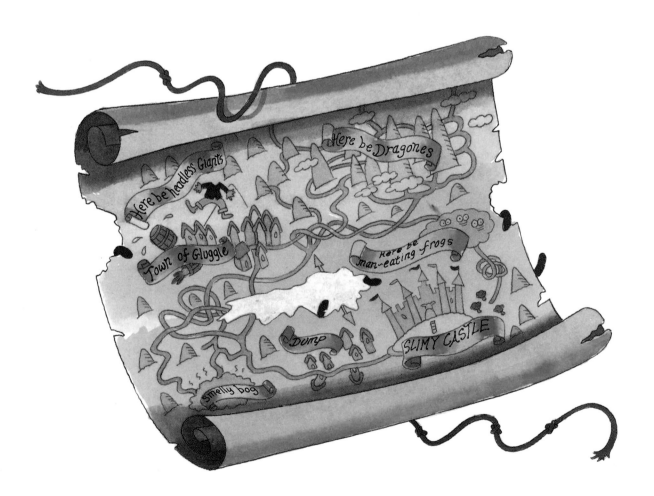

Sir Bertilak's impatience grew as the rain continued to fall, especially when it began to fall *inside* the castle. The roof had not been repaired for centuries. Why bother when you can simply order a minion to stand under each hole with a bucket? However, when drips become torrents, even the most willing minion with the biggest bucket is no use. Sir Bertilak cowered under a canopy and growled.

When the rain slowed to a few sulky drops, the Odorous one summoned his men and informed them that he wished to be ready to set out in an hour's time. He set his hourglass to underline the point. Sixty minutes later, the expedition, somewhat hastily prepared, set off. Needless to say, a number of essential items were left behind in the rush.

One of them was the map.

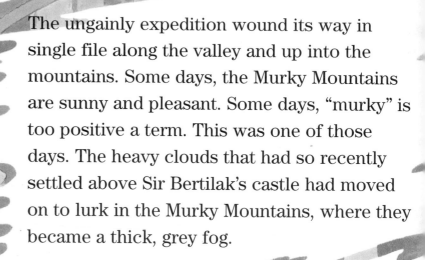

The ungainly expedition wound its way in single file along the valley and up into the mountains. Some days, the Murky Mountains are sunny and pleasant. Some days, "murky" is too positive a term. This was one of those days. The heavy clouds that had so recently settled above Sir Bertilak's castle had moved on to lurk in the Murky Mountains, where they became a thick, grey fog.

The mountain pathways were narrow. The mountain sides were steep. The number of minions with which Sir Bertilak set out rapidly dropped as those self same minions literally dropped off the side of the path. With rapidly fading yells, they disappeared from this story for ever.

Before long, the paths became even narrower. Through the foul mist, the occasional *clang* was heard, as, one by one, the brave leader's armed men also fell off the winding way and bounced gently down the mountainside.

It was late afternoon, and growing even darker, when Sir Bertilak suddenly noticed that only he and Porrit remained of the motley crew that had set out. Sir Bertilak was too stupid to realize that he should be panicking. Porrit was too intelligent to tell him.

"I suggest, sire," he ventured, "that we should rest in this cave until … until the rest of the party catches up with us."

"Sluggards!" sneered Sir Bertilak loudly. "Laggards! Slaggards!"

Porrit hurried his master into the cave before he could do any more damage to the English language.

It was surprisingly warm inside the cave. It was surprisingly light, too—almost as if there was a glow coming from the back of the rocky shelter.

Sir Bertilak, rapidly shedding clothes until an unwholesome amount of his flabby flesh was visible, began to rant about the subject that was always uppermost in his mind: dragons.

"Of course," he pontificated, "we might meet one at any time, but the likelihood is that they are all hiding. It's well known that dragons are lily-livered overgrown lizards, scared to show their faces when humans are around. They are cowardly creatures. No wonder it takes a man of my skills to hunt one down."

At some point during this speech, Porrit began to gesticulate wildly and make funny sounds in the back of his throat. Sir Bertilak took no notice, although he did begin to feel even hotter.

"Dragons aren't the creatures they're cracked up to be," the knight went on. "They're only slimy reptiles, after all. As for fire-breathing, well, I've seen circus tricksters do it. It's nothing to get worked up about."

In the next second, three important things happened. There was something that sounded very like a snort of derision. Sir Bertilak yelped as his greasy locks caught fire. And Porrit fainted.

The dragon, who had been sitting quietly in the back of the cave for some time, watched with amusement as Sir Bertilak rushed outside and stuck his head into a convenient mountain pool. She looked down with interest at young Porrit, who smelt vaguely familiar, before lolloping gently into the depths of the cave, leaving the intrepid hunters in the dark in more ways than one.

"Absolutely no need," growled the knight with the singed locks, "to mention this to anyone at all."

"Sorry, sire," said Porrit diplomatically. "I fainted and didn't see a thing. What did happen, exactly?"

"I was hit by lightning," said Sir Bertilak, in a flash (as it were) of inspiration. "That's very rare, you know. It marks you out from the crowd."

In Sir Bertilak's case, it certainly did. From that day, he sported a decidedly dodgy hair-do, which no amount of grooming could ever improve.

Boiled!

Sir Bertilak Odorous and young Porrit spent the night in the cave. It seemed wiser than venturing out into fog that became murkier with every passing minute. The page did not sleep at all. Having had a good look at the unseen inhabitant of the rocky room, he felt that someone at least should keep watch. Sir Bertilak, who had now persuaded himself of the truth of his lightning story, had no such inhibitions. He snored happily through the night until a small boulder hit him heavily on the nose.

he would-be dragon-slayer was dazed for a moment. Then he
apt to his feet and shook his page vigorously.

Not a very funny joke, Porrit!" he snarled, as his
ose swelled to twice its usual size.

n balance, Porrit thought it better to take the
lame than to reveal that a scalier hand than
is own had probably thrown the missile.
esides, dawn was breaking on a crisp,
ear day. It was time to go home.

he pair set off down the narrow path. Sir Bertilak grumbled and groaned without pause.
orrit was silent. Several important thoughts were chasing each other through his tired
rain and causing him deep concern. Firstly,
here was the narrowness of the path.
esterday, in the fog, Porrit had been
lissfully unaware of the yawning
hasms at his feet. Now, every
tep seemed to cause him to
way dangerously over the edge.

Secondly, there was the serious problem of his master and his master's obsession. Porrit knew that once Sir Bertilak had an idea, he would not rest until it was achieved. Whatever you might want to say about the knight's morals, hygiene, or social graces, you had to give him full marks for persistence. It was the kind of quality that had enabled Sir Bertilak's ancestors to trample the peasantry underfoot on their way to the top. Sir Bertilak had decided to be a famous dragon-slayer, and he would not rest until at least one dragon was slain.

Porrit had mixed feelings. He had now had two-and-a-half (if you count the boulder-throwing incident) encounters with dragons, and he was beginning to have a sneaking respect for the creatures. It occurred to him that a dragon who was not exercising considerable restraint would have scorched more than Sir Bertilak's hair. Indeed, you might have expected two human beings sharing a cave overnight with a dragon to have been found toasted if not roasted. Porrit wondered why he was alive at all.

It was even stranger that the obnoxious Odorous one, whose views on dragons were hardly politically correct, had only a silly haircut to show for a night in the mountains.

Porrit was a loyal page. He followed his master through thick (no one could say that Sir Bertilak was the brightest button in the box) and thin (gruel, mostly). But Porrit's mind was much occupied, which is perhaps why, when he looked up, he was shocked to see that Sir Bertilak was no longer stomping along in front of him.

In horror, Porrit peered over the edge of the ledge. Surely he would have heard a body as solid as Sir B's thudding down the slope? It was hard to believe that the knight would have gone quietly. The page was forced to conclude that his master had taken a different path. Porrit turned around and, as quickly as he dared, retraced hissteps around the mountainside.

It wasn't long before a strange sulphurous smell began to tickle his nostrils. It smelt as if something rotten was being burnt. Dread filled Porrit's humble heart. To be honest, it wasn't really that he feared for the health of Sir Bertilak. It was more that he felt a little squeamish about the sight that might meet his eyes. Sir Bertilak had, on more than one occasion, regaled his page with the story of how he had discovered his overcooked uncle outside a dragon's lair. The details had been gruesome in the extreme.

Porrit steeled himself to turn the next bend, behind which billows of smoke were wafting. Coughing and spluttering, he clung to the rock and prepared himself for a ghastly sight.

It was a ghastly sight indeed. A naked Sir Bertilak was cavorting in a steaming pool, fed by warm springs. His clothing, flung over nearby rocks, decorated the scene. Porrit gulped and averted his eyes. It was several months since Sir Bertilak had bathed. In the hot water and steam, his hairy hide had become the colour of a cooked lobster—but nothing like so appetizing.

"Come on in!" yelled Sir Bertilak. "And you can wash my clothes while you're about it!"

Porrit dutifully obeyed, but sensibly jumped in fully clad. He figured that his own clothes could get washed at the same time. Porrit laboured for hours on Sir Bertilak's ghastly garments, while his master plunged and wallowed like a demented whale.

At last, with the clothes draped over the rocks to dry, Porrit sat down on the edge of the pool and, worn out after his sleepless night, fell fast asleep.

He was rudely awoken by bellowing. Sir Bertilak had lumbered from the water and was searching for his clothes. They were nowhere to be seen.

This time, Porrit hesitated to take the blame. Among the many pleasant things that Sir Bertilak was in the process of promising the perpetrator, being held upside-down in the steaming pool was one of the most appealing.

Porrit cleared his throat. "It is well known, Sire," he said, "that dragons often steal the clothes of those they fear. They hope it will diminish their strength and power."

Sir Bertilak paused in mid-rant. "Really?" he muttered. A silly smile spread across his face. "Porrit," he grinned, "we're getting somewhere at last! I can *smell* success! Let's get home and make proper preparations."

The pair trudged towards the castle. The broiled baron was no longer grumbling but humming happily (horribly, but happily) to himself. Porrit was dodging from rock to rock. One of the pair would be arriving home naked. You can bet your own buttocks it wasn't Sir Bertilak.

Roasted!

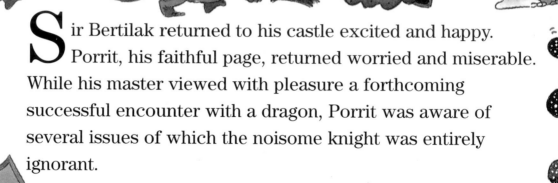

Sir Bertilak returned to his castle excited and happy. Porrit, his faithful page, returned worried and miserable. While his master viewed with pleasure a forthcoming successful encounter with a dragon, Porrit was aware of several issues of which the noisome knight was entirely ignorant.

    1. There were not just one or two dragons in the vicinity. The Murky Mountains were crawling with them.

    2. The dragons were not, as Sir Bertilak believed, stupid and cowardly. They were clever and courageous.

    3. Sir Bertilak was not, as he himself believed, clever and courageous. He was stupid and rashly stupid.

    4. (And this was the worst point of all.) The dragons had a tremendous sense of humour.

While Sir Bertilak spent an uncomfortable couple of hours being squidged and squeezed into a new suit of clothes, Porrit sat on the least smelly bit of floor he could find and thought about everything that had happened. It didn't increase his cheeriness. When his master finally stomped into the room, his first words made Porrit feel even worse.

"Porrit!" roared Sir Bertilak, "I've had a thought!"

These unlikely words would make any page tremble. With growing terror, Porrit listened while his master expounded his peculiar ponderings.

"I've been thinking about the old stories, Porrit," said Sir Bertilak, sitting down heavily on an unsuspecting hound. "There's a lot of sense in some of those ancient tales. Do you know what we've been missing in all our quests?"

Several words sprang to mind. Intelligence? Common sense? Hygiene?
"No, sire," muttered Porrit.

"That's why you're a paltry page and I'm a knight," replied Sir Bertilak with satisfaction. "The answer is staring you in the face. At least, it isn't staring you in the face. And that's the problem."

"You mean…?" enquired Porrit, totally at sea but hoping he sounded as if he was understanding every word.

"Maidens!" hollered Sir Bertilak. "All the legends of the past have a maiden in them. You chain her up on a rock and, when the dragon turns up and eats her, you leap out and kill it."

"I think you're supposed to kill it *before* it eats the maiden," squawked Porrit. "Before? After? What's the difference?" cried his master. "Now, who have we got we could chain to a rock?"

In truth, Sir Bertilak's history with maidens or any self-respecting woman had not been glorious. Most of them had the sense to keep out of his way. There was, in fact, only one suitable unfortunate female in the castle. Porrit shut his eyes and prayed that his master would not think of the obvious. It was to no avail.

"Agnes!" screeched Sir Bertilak. "Perfect! It's time that wretched girl made herself useful."

I should explain that Agnes was Sir Bertilak's niece, dumped on him by his brother, a knight second only to Sir B in general awfulness. Sir Slimeone had gone off to fight in the crusades (a hundred and fifty years after they were over). As his map-reading was as bad as his grasp of current affairs, he had sailed off in entirely the wrong direction. His arrival in North America is unrecorded by the history books, as is his encounter with an unfriendly bear—a meeting that could only be described as grisly.

Agnes was a sensible girl and did her best to avoid the notice of her uncle. She had not, however, avoided the notice of Porrit, who was inclined to think that she was the most angelic creature ever to place her perfumed foot upon the blossoming earth. (She did not, in fact, have perfumed feet—far from it—but that was the way Porrit thought about her.)

Porrit was panicking now. He begged Sir Bertilak to consider the foul mood Sir Slimeone might be in if he returned to find his daughter roasted by a reptile. The knight was not impressed. Out of sight was out of mind in his book, and anyway, he thought it unlikely that his brother would ever return. In this he was, very unusually, correct. Before Porrit could think of another argument, the protesting girl was dragged before her uncle.

"Agnes," said Sir Bertilak with a smile that struck horror into the hearts of all that saw it, "I thought we might go for a little picnic in the country. Let's see. Where would be pleasant at this time of year? Hmmm. Oh, I know! The Murky Mountains! Go and get your cloak, my dear."

Agnes was a level-headed and intelligent girl. If the gruesome leer on her uncle's face and the unexpectedness of the invitation had not worried her, the sight of Porrit, pale and trembling as if he had seen a ghost, would have alarmed her a great deal. Thoughtfully, she returned to her chamber and tucked a number of potentially useful items into her clothing before joining her uncle in the courtyard.

The picnic party set out. Agnes wondered why her uncle felt it necessary to wear full armour. She wondered why the mule carrying the food made a clanking sound as it walked. She wondered why Porrit, who usually gazed at her with pitiful adoration, now couldn't look at her at all. Agnes tightened her grip on a small dagger hidden up her sleeve and kept her wits about her.

For once the Murky Mountains were anything but murky. The sun beat down as th
small party, consisting of Sir Bertilak, Agnes, Porrit and a couple of men-at-arm
wound its way through the foothills. By the time the party had reached the highe
peaks, Sir Bertilak was positively steaming. The heat and the suit of armour resulte
in a kind of pressure-cooker effect. He felt more and more uncomfortable.

"It's no good," came a muffled roar at last, "I can't keep this stuff on I'll roast in her
Let me out!"

Porrit knew that it would take some time to extricate big Sir B from his armour.
This might be the only chance. He casually wandered past Agnes on her palfry and
whispered out of the side of his mouth, "Watch for your chance. Escape! Go!"

"What?" asked Agnes. "Speak up, I can't hear you!"

Porrit raised his voice a fraction and added to it an expression of such doleful pleading that there was no doubting his meaning. Agnes was no fool. She gripped her reins and prepared for flight. Meanwhile, Porrit was beginning to wrestle with Sir Bertilak's helmet. "Now!" he yelled.

Alas, the shout, Agnes's enthusiastic kicks and the heat of the day had a bad effect on the paltry palfry. It neighed. It reared. It kicked out with all four feet and took off at the speed of light down a mountain track no wider than Agnes's unperfumed foot. Meanwhile, two men-at-arms, a hapless page and an over-armed knight, having been heavily hit by a flying hoof each, flew through the air with the greatest of ease. Where will they fall? Will Agnes become a dragon's dinner? Do belligerent Bertilaks bounce? For the answer to these and many other questions, turn to page 122.

Simmered!

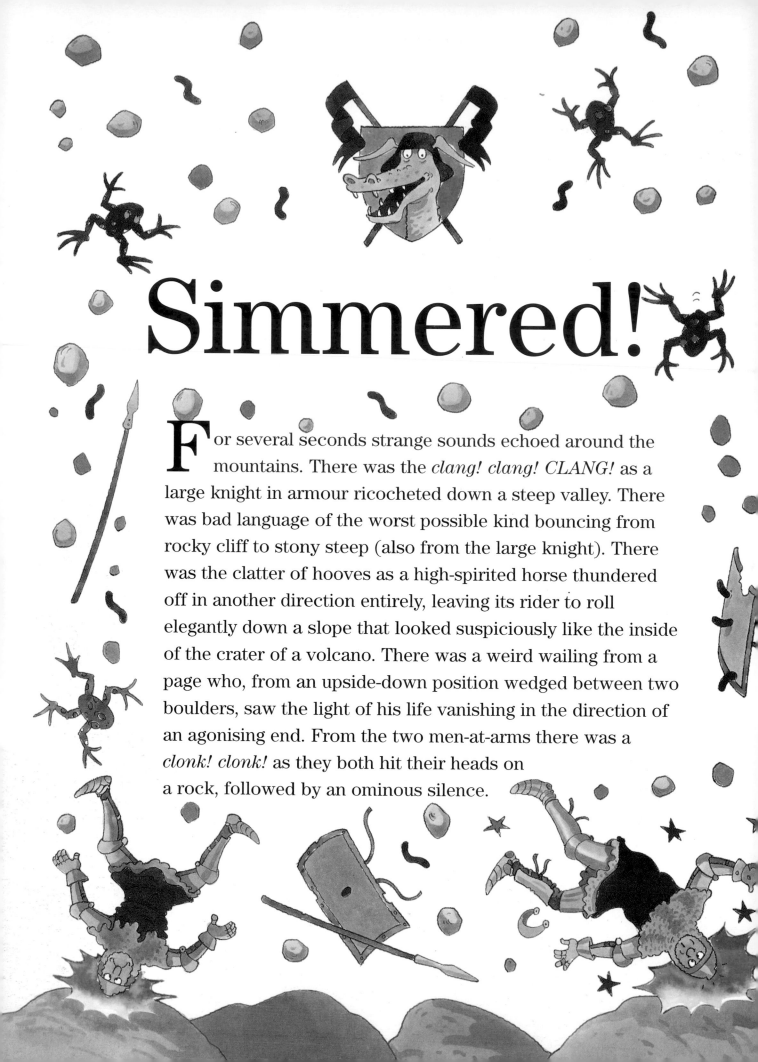

For several seconds strange sounds echoed around the mountains. There was the *clang! clang! CLANG!* as a large knight in armour ricocheted down a steep valley. There was bad language of the worst possible kind bouncing from rocky cliff to stony steep (also from the large knight). There was the clatter of hooves as a high-spirited horse thundered off in another direction entirely, leaving its rider to roll elegantly down a slope that looked suspiciously like the inside of the crater of a volcano. There was a weird wailing from a page who, from an upside-down position wedged between two boulders, saw the light of his life vanishing in the direction of an agonising end. From the two men-at-arms there was a *clonk! clonk!* as they both hit their heads on a rock, followed by an ominous silence.

As the echoes faded away with a *clang! pustules! clop! wah! clonk!* Porrit unwedged himself with difficulty and waited while the blood rushed back to his boots. In such a situation, a page's duty is to his master. Porrit knew perfectly well that what he *should* do was to clamber carefully down to the ledge far below where he could see something like a large, shiny beetle waving its legs in the air. At any moment, Sir Bertilak might become dislodged and plummet to his doom.

Porrit, as we know, was a faithful page, but his heart was hurtling down a volcano with the woman of his dreams and he had to follow it. Ignoring the bellowing beetle below, he set off down a perilous path towards dark and steamy depths.

Meanwhile, Agnes was having a rather interesting time. As she rolled towards certain death, her skirts caught on an outcrop of rock. She found herself inelegantly hanging just above the entrance to a cave. By swinging and wriggling, she eventually managed to tear herself free from her skirts and drop down into the mouth of the cave.

At first sight, the cave appeared to be empty, but an eerie glow towards the back encouraged the intrepid maiden to explore. As she crept forward, she was surprised to hear, faintly at first, then louder and louder, an extraordinary kind of music.

Five hundred years before its appearance among human beings, rock and roll was wildly popular among dragons. (It was named, of course, after the round stony stuff they found all around them and what happened if you gave it a hearty shove down a mountainside.)

Agnes peered around a corner, her eardrums pulsating, and found herself in a vast cavern, where four dragons were entertaining an excessively excited crowd of young reptiles.

Meanwhile, back on the ledge, or rather, on his back on the ledge, Sir Bertilak, who earlier, you remember, had felt unwelcomingly warm in his armour, was now positively poached. The sun shone down on his shiny breastplate, toasting his tummy within. The knight grew hotter and hotter, and crosser and crosser. He hollered for his page until he was hoarse. He swore and cursed until the rocks around him turned red. But no one came.

Sir Bertilak, unable to see anything but the searing sky above him through the visor of his helmet, which had wedged shut, had no idea that he was lying on a very narrow ledge. The ledge was, in fact, a good deal more narrow than the knight. If he had known, Sir Bertilak might not have wriggled so wrathfully…

CLANG! CLUNK! KER-CLONG! BOING! SPLASSSSHHHHHH! Sir Bertilak jiggled himself off his ledge and descended a thousand feet or so at astonishing speed. At the bottom, he found himself sitting in a small mountain pool of delicious coolness. Steam rose around him as he quietly (for once) cooled. His helmet had come off in the fall (Sir Bertilak made a mental note to have his armourer's guts of garters in an all-too-literal sense), and a broad smile filled the knight's foolish face as he felt coolness reach parts that had been disturbingly simmered.

Life for Porrit was less blissful at that moment. His skirts being shorter than Agnes's, he did not get caught on the protruding rock but instead knocked first his knee and then his head with a sickening thwack. He felt as if he were falling from a great height (well, he *was* falling from a great height but he now felt it even more), and the world suddenly went black.

A couple of hundred feet further into the mountain, Agnes was crouching behind a rock and observing the scene before her. She hardly knew what to feel most shocked about—the sight of a huge group of dragons (when she had never seen a single one in her life before) or the sound of rock and roll (when she had only ever heard tedious troubador songs and Sir Bertilak's hunting bellows before). It was a lot for a girl to take in.

Just as Agnes's heart was beginning to thump a little less (it may, in any case, have been confused with the driving beat being laid down by the dragons' drummer), she found she had something worse to worry about. A large hand was placed firmly on her shoulder and she felt hot breath on the back of her neck.

For an awful moment, Agnes thought that Sir Bertilak had caught up with her. She looked down. In an even more awful moment, she realized that the hand was distinctly scaly.

Agnes, as you know, had no experience of dealing with dragons. Swiftly, she reviewed her options:

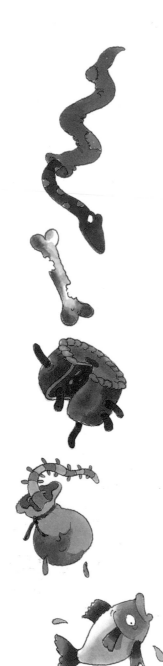

1. She could stab the creature with her dagger or any one of the other small implements she had brought with her.

2. She could try to engage the dragon in conversation and appeal to its better instincts.

3. She could fall down and pretend to be dead.

Just as swiftly, Agnes dismissed the first two options.

1. Her dagger was very small. The dragon was very large. It would be like stabbing Sir Bertilak with a darning needle. It wouldn't kill him and it wouldn't do much for his temper.

2. She had no idea if dragons understood English. Worse, she had no idea if dragons had better instincts.

The dragon leaned over and looked into Agnes's face. He sighed, singeing the maiden's eyebrows.
Agnes had no need to choose option 3.
She fainted, and it chose
itself.

What is not generally known is that dragons often have as little experience of how to deal with maidens as maidens have of how to deal with dragons.

The dragon thought a bit and looked closely at Agnes, singeing more of her hair in the process.

He wondered if she was cold, and breathed even more heavily, completing the singeing process.

Finally, he picked her up and carried her off to a cool cave where she would keep fresh while he consulted his mother.

It was only a few minutes before Agnes awoke. She felt a little chillier. She would have felt chillier still if she had known she was in the dragon equivalent of a fridge.

It was gloomy in the cave. Agnes waited until her eyes grew used to the dark and noticed a lumpy shape on the other side of the space. The longer she sat in the silence, the more convinced she became that the lumpy shape was breathing, but with her ears still throbbing from the dragons' disco, she couldn't be sure.There was only one thing to do. Agnes crawled cautiously across the cave, peering through the gloom. It looked like … it couldn't be … it was strangely like…

"Aaaaaaaaaaaaaagh!" screamed Agnes, startled by a badly bruised Porrit.

"Aaaaaaaaaaaaaagh!" screeched Porrit, horrified by a terribly toasted Agnes.

When they had regained their composure, the hapless pair explained to each other what had happened since they had last been together. It seemed like hours ago but was, in fact, a mere seven minutes.

Porrit was trembling with relief that his beloved had been found, even if her hairstyle was now a little extreme, but he suddenly found himself breathless and red in the face.

"What is it?" asked Agnes. "Are you going to faint?"

"N-n-n-n-no," stammered Porrit. "It's … it's … you're showing your l-l-l-legs!" He had never seen a maiden's legs before and felt strongly that he shouldn't be seeing them now."

"Oh, for goodness sake!" cried Agnes, when she realised what the problem was. "How did you think I got around?"

This interesting conversation was rudely interrupted by the arrival of the dragon who had found Agnes and his mother, not best plessed to be dragged away from her dancing.

Now dragons speak a very ancient language. It combines prehistoric grunts and squeals with a high-pitched wailing. What is not generally known is that after hundreds of years of rock and roll, most dragons have hardly any hearing left at all. Although the grunts and squeals still go on, they mainly communicate by lip-reading.

Porrit and Agnes cowered in a corner while the dragon and his mother made extraordinary noises at each other. The cave was, of course, no longer gloomy, as the fiery breath of the related reptiles gave an eerie red glow.

The humans had no idea what was being said, which was probably just as well. Here is a translation.

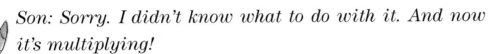

Mother: You dragged me away for THIS?

Son: Sorry. I didn't know what to do with it. And now it's multiplying!

Mother: What are you talking about? I threw this other one in here myself five minutes ago. It fell on me on my way to the concert. It wasn't awake then.

Son: So what are we going to do with them?

Mother: Humans are pretty feeble. If we leave them here they'll start to go off. We can eat them or throw them into the volcano.

Son: Do they taste good?

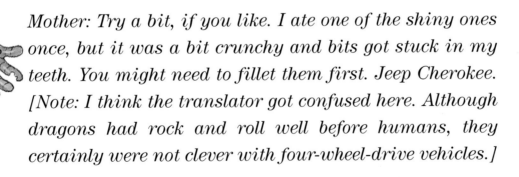

Mother: Try a bit, if you like. I ate one of the shiny ones once, but it was a bit crunchy and bits got stuck in my teeth. You might need to fillet them first. Jeep Cherokee. [Note: I think the translator got confused here. Although dragons had rock and roll well before humans, they certainly were not clever with four-wheel-drive vehicles.]

Son: Oh, let's just leave them. It sounds like too much trouble.

Mother: Boom, chugga, boom, chugga, wah, wah, wah. Come ON! This is my favourite song...

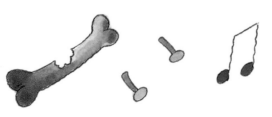

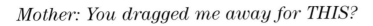
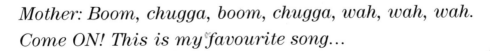

With that, the dragons waddled away.

"Let's get out of here," said Porrit, which was the most sensible thing he had said for some time. Hand in hand, he and Agnes crept out of the cave.

Ever been lost in a mountain? The pair wisely turned away from the throbbing of the bass beat, but that meant they were wandering deeper into the cave system. This would have been even more difficult if Agnes had not retrieved a flint and a torch from somewhere about her person. By its weak and flickering light, they went on.

There were curious drawings on the walls, from which Agnes and Porrit might have learnt much if they had stopped to look at them. There were horrible rumblings and hissings from underground vents. There were stalagmites and stalactites placed exactly at forehead and big-toe height.

At last, glimmering in the distance, a faint light appeared. Agnes and Porrit quickened their pace. To the page's disappointment, Agnes let go of his hand and strode on ahead. Seeing, quite literally, the light at the end of the tunnel had raised her spirits.

The entrance, when they reached it, was bathed in bright sunshine. Porrit and Agnes blinked and for a moment were unable to see where they were. Then an all-too-familiar voice boomed out from somewhere horribly close.

"Ye snipes and little swillins, what have you done to yourself, girl? No dragon's going to want you now!"

It was Sir Bertilak Odorous, sitting on a rock above a pool with his armour gently rusting into a kind of shell. He was hungry. He was angry. He was no further forward in his mission. In short, he needed someone to blame. As usual, Porrit was perfect.

Poached!

The language used by Sir Bertilak Odorous to his unfortunate page was appalling. He ignored the presence of Agnes, who would have raised her eyebrows at some of the words used if she had still had eyebrows. More to the point, the noisome knight ignored the presence of dragons. Of course, he was the only member of the company who still hadn't met a dragon, but all that was very shortly to change…

High above, among the rocky peaks, a couple of dragons we have met before were taking the air. It would never have occurred to them to peer down into the deep crevice beneath if it hadn't been for the booming and badgering coming from below. Dragons, as you know, do not hear well, but Sir Bertilak was venting his anger at a vicious volume. Furthermore, the crevice acted as a kind of natural megaphone, funnelling the sound to the ears of the scaly ones above.

I will spare you the words of Sir Bertilak. (It would not, in any case, be legal for me to print them on this page.) The words of the dragons, however, can safely be recorded. Again, the following passage is a translation.

Son: Hey! Look down there! Isn't that...?

Mother: Hmmm. Maybe. But you're right. They do seem to be multiplying. The baby looks huge. And it's one of the shiny ones. No good to us at all.

Son: Why does it have to make so much noise?

Mother: Babies are like that. Look, I'm fed up with this. Use your initiative. Make it stop.

The younger dragon considered for a moment scrambling down the rocky crevice and flame-grilling the humans, but it seemed like too much effort. Instead, he picked up a handy rock and threw it into the depths.

None of the humans below heard the approaching missile, but Porrit chose that moment to seize his belovéd and cover her ears, thereby pulling her out of the line of fire. A second later, Sir Bertilak felt the full force of the reptile's rock. It volleyed from his vambrace; it bounced from his breastplate; it pounded painfully on one of his poleyns.

Boing! Bong! Bing!

Sir Bertilak was too shocked to speak for a moment, but far above, the dragons had become strangely interested.

Son: Did you hear that? It sounded great! Banana laundry!
[Sorry. Another translation problem, I think. Presumably this is some kind of slang Dragonese that is difficult to convey in modern English.]

Mother: You're right. Try it again.

Another rock followed the first and hurtled into the depths. This time, it ricocheted from Sir Bertilak's rotund tummy, veered back onto the vambrace and plopped even more painfully down to his pulsating poleyn.

Bong! Boing! Bing!

Sir Bertilak's fury knew no bounds. The adjectives he used about avalanches were utterly awful. But his excitement didn't begin to match that of the lizardlike listeners above.

Son: That's fantastic! It's just what we've been looking for.
A brilliant new sound!

Mother: I can't wait to hear more!

And she did. Thirty-four rocks of various sizes came hurtling
down the mountain. After the first nine, Sir Bertilak became
strangely quiet, and Porrit and Agnes hid their eyes.

A symphony of sounds filled the Murky Mountains and suddenly
the sound of enthusiastic applause echoed through the valleys.
Porrit and Agnes looked up and saw to their astonishment that
every ledge was packed with dragons, all drawn to the percussive
sound of rocks hitting rogue.

Porrit's knees were shaking, but he felt he should try to be masterful.

"Don't move," he whispered to his true love, holding her close.

"Stop spitting in my ears!" hissed Agnes, who was far too interested in the dragons to feel the romance of the situation.

Neither Porrit nor Agnes needed to worry. Focussing on the best bit of drum kit to make its way to the Murky Mountains for many a millennium, the dragons took no notice at all of a couple of cowering humans. Several of them clambered down to Sir Bertilak's rock and lifted him off it, being particularly careful not to breathe on any part that looked as though it might be tuneful. As Porrit and Agnes watched, open-mouthed, the rapacious reptiles bore Sir Bertilak, now moaning faintly, away. The last they saw of him was the glint of his greaves as he was carried into a cave.

Not a scrap of scaly skin, not a hint of horny head, not a flicker of flaring flame remained to be seen. Porrit and Agnes looked around. Then they looked at each other.

"Did that," murmured Porrit, "really happen?"

Agnes nodded. "Look!"

Lying by the pool was Sir Bertilak's much-bashed helmet, which he had removed when the sun beat down. Porrit picked it up.

"We should go and look for him," he said. "I'm sure *The Page's Handbook* would say it was my duty to rescue my master from danger of every kind.

Probably," he went on miserably, "that includes kidnap by dragons."

"Probably," Agnes agreed flatly. The pair exchanged a long and meaningful look. Neither spoke but a great deal was going on in both their minds. Agnes was thinking, "Porrit wouldn't look bad in a blue jerkin. I wonder where my uncle hid my jewels? It's probably much too late to save him now. I'm hungry." (Remember, she *was* related to the nasty nobleman.)

Porrit was thinking, "Your eyes are like pools of sparkling sapphire. I wonder if you'd clonk me on the head if I said so. It's probably much too late to save him now. I'm hungry." (Remember, he'd had a very trying day.)

And so, hand in hand, Agnes and Porrit began the long walk back to the castle, feeling, although neither said a word, curiously in tune. And, speaking of tunes, if their thoughts had not been elsewhere, they might have heard, wafting through the valleys, a strangely melodious sound:

The Troll and the Billy Goats

Once upon a time, there were three billy goats who loved to eat fresh, green grass. Does this sound familiar? You probably already know the story of the three billy goats Gruff. At least, you know the story the billy goats told. The poor old troll, floating off down the river, never got a chance to tell his side of the tale. Now, this is what really happened.

Trolls, as you know, are usually only interested in one thing—gold. They spend all day long digging in the earth, or wading in streams, trying to find gleaming nuggets of the precious metal.

Even if a troll has piles and piles of gold stored in a cave somewhere (and some of them do), he never feels he has enough. He carries on digging until the end of his days.

The troll in this story was just like that. He spent his life panning for gold in the mountain streams. One sunny day, when he was working away near an old wooden bridge, he suddenly saw something glittering in the sand at the bottom of his pan. It was gold!

Chortling with glee, the troll held the pan up high and let the sunlight sparkle on his find.

Just at that moment . . . *Trip trap!*
Trip trap! Trip trap!

A tiny billy goat came stomping over the bridge, making an incredible amount of noise with his tiny hoofs. Startled by the noise, the troll dropped his pan—and the gold that was in it—right back into the river.

Not surprisingly, he gave a howl of rage. And the tiny billy goat, thinking this sounded very much like a creature who might want to eat something small and furry, scuttled off to the other side of the bridge.

The troll grunted and growled. He had never eaten a goat in his life and didn't intend to start now, but he certainly didn't feel very friendly towards anything with horns and a silly white beard.

After a few moments, the troll's mind went back to what was really important to him. You know what that was. Patiently, he retrieved his pan and started dipping it into the stream once more.

He was unbelievably lucky. Once again, something gleamed at the bottom. With a crow of delight, the troll peered at the glittering gold. This time he was taking no chances. Very, very carefully, he swooshed away the sand and grit. Then he tipped the tiny grains of gold into a leather purse he kept in his pocket for just this purpose.

But just at that moment…
Trip trap! Trip trap!
Trip trap!

The middle-sized billy goat Gruff came galloping across the bridge, making a dreadful din.

The troll dropped his purse. It went plop! into the water and disappeared. This time the troll was not so restrained. He gave a huge bellow and thrust his head over the edge of the bridge, frightening the middle-sized billy goat a great deal. The creature dashed off over the bridge, convinced that a monster was about to gobble him up whole.

The poor old troll stuck his head under the water and looked about for the purse. It was a brownish shade, very much like the rocks in the stream. Every so often he came up for air, his face red and dripping.

When the troll's gnarled fingers closed around the bag at last, he breathed a sigh of relief, forgetting he was under water. Streams of bubbles made him cough and splutter. He reared up into the air, with water streaming from him, looking quite horrifying.

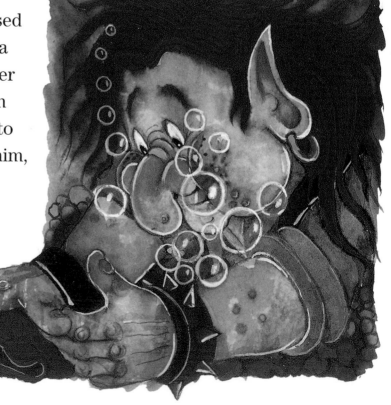

In one swift movement, the troll heaved himself up onto the bridge—just as the largest billy goat Gruff came thundering across it. *Trip trap!* *TRIP TRAP!* *TRIP TRAP!*

Woomph! The billy goat wasn't looking where he was going. Quite by accident, his horns made contact with the poor old troll. He'd already had a hard day. Now he flew up into the air and landed with a mighty splash in the water. Unable to find his feet, he floated off down the stream, shrieking and waving his fists. (Yes, he had lost the purse of gold *again*.)

The billy goat was dazed by the collision. Seeing something brown and plump lying on the bridge, he promptly ate it.

So next time you are told the story of the three billy goats Gruff, don't believe everything you hear. And next time you are walking over a wooden bridge, please do it very, very *quietly*.

Beware of the Ogre!

There are ogres who are only slightly unpleasant. They don't wash their hair (or anything else!) as often as they might. Their fingernails are long and pointy. They like to trip people and run off with their shopping bags. They are a nuisance and best avoided.

But there is another kind of ogre who is much, much more worrying. He will eat anything he finds (including cats and grandmothers). He will jump out at you when you least expect it. He is the kind of ogre your mother always warned you about.

It was the second kind of ogre that lived in the dark forest near the village of Mingle, so people said. At one time, Mingle was a happy place, where elves went about their business singing and little children played outside their homes. But ever since the ogre came to live nearby, things had changed.

At night, mother elves would sing to their children:

> *Little ones,*
> *Close your eyes,*
> *Grow up happy,*
> *Healthy and wise.*
> *But never go near*
> *the forest. Beware!*
> *A horrible, terrible*
> *Ogre lives there!*

Yes, the elves of Mingle were frightened. They felt that they couldn't go into the forest for picnics any more. Worse still, they felt that they couldn't go into the forest for firewood. The first winter after the ogre arrived was a very cold one. The little elves shivered in their homes and pulled the bedclothes up to their chins.

By the time winter was almost over, the elves were miserable and too scared to set foot outside the village. Sometimes if you are very frightened, it's hard to think straight. That is exactly what had happened to the elves.

Then, one fine day, a troll came marching through the village on his way to the mines. He noticed right away that something was wrong, and although elves don't like trolls very much either, they found themselves telling him the whole story.

"We know the ogre is still there," said old Mrs. Mumm, "because we can see the smoke from his fire."

"So," grunted the troll, "he's one of the worst kind, is he?"

"The very worst," said Mrs. Mumm.

"Worse than worst," said Mr. Pringle, her cousin.

"I don't want to open up old wounds," said the troll, "but what sort of thing has he done?"

The elves all spoke at once.

"He frightened my cow, so she wouldn't give any milk for a week!"

"He ate one of my chickens … unless it ran away!"

"He pulled up all my cabbages and half my carrots!"

"And we haven't seen a single squirrel since he arrived," added Mrs. Mumm darkly.

"Wait a minute. Let me get this straight," muttered the troll. "He hasn't eaten any children. He hasn't eaten any grandmothers. He hasn't even eaten any cats. He helped himself to one chicken—maybe—and some vegetables. That's bad, of course, but it's not very, very bad, is it?"

"Don't forget the squirrels," said Mrs. Mumm.

"It's winter," the troll replied patiently. "All self-respecting squirrels are tucked up in their beds asleep, waiting for spring to come. I'm not saying this ogre isn't a nasty piece of work. I'm saying you don't really know. Why don't we try to find out?"

Mrs. Mumm strode forward. "I'll do it!" she cried. "And what's more, I've got a plan."

Mrs. Mumm's plan was this. She would take a large basket of food to the very edge of the forest and sit down as if to have a picnic. If the ogre came out and stole the food to eat, they would know that he was not so bad after all. If he came out and stole Mrs. Mumm to eat, it would be a different story.

The troll looked at Mrs. Mumm with admiration.

"It's a bit risky," he said. "Are you sure?"

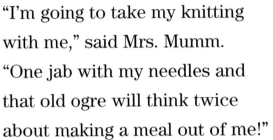

"I'm going to take my knitting with me," said Mrs. Mumm. "One jab with my needles and that old ogre will think twice about making a meal out of me!"

So Mrs. Mumm filled her basket and off she went.

As many of the villagers as could manage—and the visiting troll—climbed up into the church steeple with Mr. Pringle's telescope to watch what happened.

"She's sitting down by the basket," reported Mr. Pringle. "Don't push, young Perkins! It's my telescope, you know!"

After that, nothing happened for a long time. Everyone got bored and started wishing they had brought sandwiches. Then, suddenly, Mr. Pringle said, "Oh my goodness!" and fell down in a faint. When young Perkins took his place at the telescope, all he could see was a piece of flattened grass.

No ogre. No basket. And no Mrs. Mumm.

"Now what do we do?" asked Mr. Pringle, when he came to. All eyes turned to the troll.

"We'd better go and find out," said the troll with a sigh. "Come on. If we all go, we can run away in lots of directions at once and confuse him."

Tottering on tiptoes, the elves and the troll crept to the edge of the forest.
As they reached the first trees, Mr. Pringle began to sniff the air.

"There's a wonderful smell," he said. "Is it roast chicken? Is it roast pork?"

A dreadful silence fell over the party.

"Is it roast Mrs. Mumm?" asked young Perkins,
who never knew when to keep quiet.

"There's only one way to find out,"
grunted the troll grimly. "Come on!"

Through the dark trees the trembling troop stumbled, growing closer and closer to the smell of something truly delicious. Then, through the trees, they saw an amazing sight.

In a clearing where a huge pot was bubbling over a fire, the ogre and old Mrs. Mumm were sitting comfortably, nibbling a variety of delicate *hors d'oeuvres*. They appeared to be discussing the finer points of pastry-making.

"Ah, there you are!" cried Mrs. Mumm, when she saw the peeping party.
"Meet my friend Horgrish!"

Horgrish was no Prince Charming. His table manners were dreadful. But he was
ferociously interested in food and could cook like a dream. Even the wariest
elves found their feet mysteriously drawn toward the steaming bowls that the
ogre was (rather untidily) filling.

That afternoon, the elves learned three things.
It's a mistake to judge by appearances.
Cool hands are needed for making pastry.
And a finely seasoned vegetable stew, eaten
in the open air in good company, can more
than make up for even the most miserable winter.

A Home for an Ogre

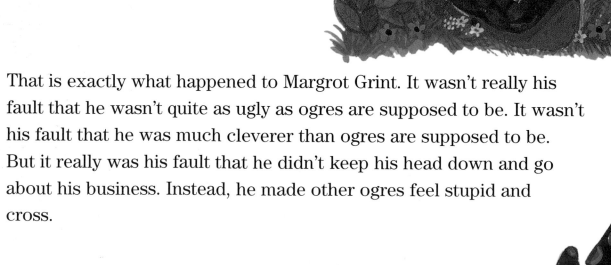

Now you don't need me to tell you that ogres are not the most popular visitors to Elfland villages. In fact, the only people who really like ogres are ogres themselves. And that is why, if an ogre falls out with his own family and friends, he is in very big trouble indeed.

That is exactly what happened to Margrot Grint. It wasn't really his fault that he wasn't quite as ugly as ogres are supposed to be. It wasn't his fault that he was much cleverer than ogres are supposed to be. But it really was his fault that he didn't keep his head down and go about his business. Instead, he made other ogres feel stupid and cross.

One fine summer's evening, for example, Margrot and some other ogres were sitting outside gazing at the stars. Even ogres have their poetic moments.

"It's amazing," said Mr. Mung, the schoolteacher. "They are so far away that no one knows exactly how far they are." "Oh yes they do," said Margrot bluntly. And he proceeded to give the whole company a lecture on astrophysics. The others didn't understand one word of it, but they couldn't help feeling that the mood of the evening had been spoiled.

It was the same when Margrot came across his old granny making ugly cakes. Now Margrot's old granny had been making ugly cakes for almost two hundred years (yes, ogres really do live that long). When her grandson began to tell her that she needed the oven to be hotter and the mixture to be colder, she didn't take kindly to his advice. The fact that he was absolutely right—and she knew it—only made matters worse.

After several years of not having the sense to keep his mouth shut, Margrot found that most ogres crossed the street when they saw him coming. Then his landlord told him that he would have to move out of his little cottage.

"It's out of my hands," said the landlord. "I'm sorry, but you'll have to go."

In vain, Margrot tried to find out what on earth he meant. The landlord turned his back and said that he would be changing the locks on Friday.

Margrot searched the whole village for a new home, but there was nothing to be had. Even his nearest and dearest seemed strangely reluctant to ask him to stay. When Friday came, Margrot found himself standing outside his old home with a bag of dirty clothes (ogres are no better at washing their clothes than they are at washing themselves) and four large volumes of tried and tested recipes. With a sigh that made the buds on a nearby rosebush shrivel, he set off to find another place to live.

It wasn't easy. Banished by his own kind, Margrot Grint soon found that he was even more disliked by the elves who lived nearby. The ones that didn't scream and run away when they saw him fell down in a faint instead. None of them greeted him warmly and asked him to move into a spare bedroom.

So it was that Margrot, like many ogres before him, set up home in the forest. It was cold in winter, full of stinging insects in summer, and the bathroom facilities left a lot to be desired. And Margrot was lonely. Even the local elves never ventured into the forest now that they knew Someone Else had taken up residence there.

But one day, as Margrot rested in the treehouse he had built in an enormous oak, he heard the sound of crying below. It was a small elfin boy, wailing and thumping a spelling book at the same time.

"What's the matter?" called Margrot. "Can I help?"

The boy jumped. "Only if you can do level nine elf spelling," he moaned. He couldn't see Margrot through the leaves, so he didn't know he was talking to an ogre.

Margrot Grint was so pleased to talk to another living soul that he did a sensible thing. He stayed in his treehouse and talked the boy through his problems without showing himself. After half an hour of careful coaching, the boy suddenly understood a lot more about spelling than he ever had before. He ran back to his village with a smug little grin.

It wasn't long before news of the "Wise Man of the Forest" spread among the elf children. Margrot found himself helping out with the homework of every child in the village. He enjoyed it—but never came down into the open.

Very, very slowly, grown-up elves also began to come for advice. Margrot gave his opinion on problems with relatives (after all, he knew all about that), composting methods (ogres are skilled at anything to do with smelliness), bread baking, basketweaving and babycare. He found that cleverness and common sense could come up with an answer to almost any problem.

Pretty soon, no one did anything without consulting the Wise Man first. Most mornings, an orderly line wound among the trees, waiting to speak to the voice in the tree.

Gradually, summer changed to autumn. The leaves began to fall.

Margrot began to worry.

The day came at last, as he knew it would, when an autumn gale, howling through the treetops, swept the last leaves from his tree. Looking up, a member of the crowd below caught a glimpse of Margrot Grint … and screamed.

Margrot had no choice. He clambered down and prepared to be rejected.

"Yes," he said, "I am an ogre. Now, I suppose, you will all run away."

But elves, unlike most ogres, are not stupid. Margrot was a very useful person to know.

"Ah, yes, hello Mr. Ogre," said the elves' mayor. "Now, about my plumbing…."

Giant Jim's Joke

There are times when the very best kind of friend to have is a giant. If your car is stuck in the mud, he will happily pull it out for you. If your chimney needs repairs, he will cheerfully hold you up at roof-height while you fix it. (Don't, whatever you do, be tempted to let a giant do the fixing himself. His fingers are large but they are not delicate. You could end up with more damage than you started with.) Yes, a giant can be very good at some things, but hopeless at others—as young Elbert Elf found out.

Elbert first made friends with Giant Jim when, as quite a small elf, he dropped his best red-and-blue ball into Lillimug Lake and it floated out of reach. Elbert was just about to start weeping and wailing when the ground around him began to shake. The fate of one red-and-blue ball didn't seem so important when the ground became as wobbly as jelly.

"What's the trouble, little chap?" boomed a voice that seemed to come out of the sky.

Elbert looked up … and up … and up … and up. Far, far above him, a friendly face beamed down.

"My name is Jim," it went on. "Shall I fetch your ball for you?"

Elbert was too surprised even to nod, but the giant waded into the lake—the water only came up to his ankles—and picked up the ball as if it was a pea.

After that, the giant and the little elf became great friends. Elbert soon realized there was no need to be afraid of the giant. He was always very careful where he put his big feet when little ones were around. What Elbert liked best was to ride around on Jim's shoulders. It was almost as good as being a giant himself.

But as Elbert grew older, he began to find some things about his friend annoying.

The main reason was that Jim, like most giants, really wasn't very clever. That didn't matter most of the time. Elbert didn't need help with his history homework—he could do that himself. But Elbert loved jokes, and he found that his giant friend simply didn't get them.

"What lies at the bottom of the sea and shivers, Jim?" asked the young elf.

"I don't know," replied Jim.

"A nervous wreck!" chortled Elbert.

"What was it nervous about?" asked Jim.

"No, no, it was a joke," Elbert tried to explain, but it was no use. In fact, if you've ever tried it, you'll know that it's pretty hard to explain why a joke is funny. It just is, somehow.

Elbert thought he might be able to teach Jim to understand jokes. He spent a lot of time explaining to him how "Knock! Knock!" jokes work. At last, he thought Jim had got it.

One day, Elbert asked Jim. "Will you remember me tomorrow?"

"Of course I will, Elbert," said Jim.

"Will you remember me in a week?"

"Of course," said Jim.

"Will you remember me in a year?"

"I'm sure I will," said Jim, "but you're not going anywhere, are you, Elbert?"

"Knock! Knock!" said Elbert.

Jim felt on safer ground. "Who's there?" he bellowed.

"See!" laughed the elf. "You've forgotten me already!"

"No, I haven't, Elbert. You said…"

"It was a joke, Jim," sighed Elbert. "But you never get them, do you? Maybe we just don't have enough in common to be best friends."

Elbert went off by himself and decided not to spend so much time with Jim. The giant lumbered back to his castle and wished he had never met the little elf. But both of them were miserable. Elbert found himself spending most of his time trying to think of a way of making everything right with his giant friend.

But in the end, it was Jim who broke the ice. One morning, as Elbert was leafing sadly through his jokebook, which suddenly didn't seem so very funny, there came a hammering at the door.

"There's only one person that could be," said Elbert's mother. "How that door stays on its hinges I'll never know."

Elbert hurried to the door. He could never ask his friend inside, for the roof of the little house only came up to the giant's knees. Outside the door was a pair of familiar legs—but something was odd.

"Jim," shouted Elbert, "you've got your shoes on the wrong feet!"

"But these are the only feet I've got!" replied Jim.

"That's not what I mean…" Elbert began, but Jim was roaring with laughter and making the windows wobble.

"It was a joke, Elbert!" he cried. "It was a joke!"

For a moment, Elbert's heart lifted. Jim had got it! He would be able to share his funniest jokes with him! But he soon found out he was wrong. Poor old Jim had found one joke that he understood. He had been rehearsing for a week to get it right (and he had driven most of his friends and relations mad in the process). It had been hard work for him, but he had done it to please his friend.

Elbert smiled sadly at his jokebook.
Somehow, he had missed Jim more than his jokes.
And, after all, one joke a year was
better than nothing.

Troll Trouble

Trolls and elves usually don't have much to do with each other. They have very little in common. Trolls think that there is really only one truly beautiful thing in the world—gold. Elves say, "But what about rainbows? What about dew on daisies? What about butterfly wings?" Trolls hear what they think of as fanciful nonsense … and snort.

Certainly Edgerley Elf had never had anything to do with trolls before he met Tuggle. It happened like this…

Edgerley lived with his ancient great-uncle until the old elf died. Then, at last, Edgerley felt able to move to a bright, new house. He had never liked the dark little cottage under the hawthorn hedge.

Edgerley's new home was his pride
and joy. It was beneath the graceful
branches of a silver birch tree. Light
streamed in through the windows
and gleamed on Edgerley's finely
polished furniture and fetching
flower arrangements. The young elf
was very happy.

Then, one morning, as Edgerley sat
eating his supper, he heard a strange
drumming sound. It seemed to be
coming from under his feet. The elf
assumed that a passing burrowing
bunny was making more noise than
usual. He hoped she wouldn't nibble
too many tree roots as she went.

Next morning, however, the noise
was worse. It sounded more like
clanging than thudding now.
Edgerley tried not to notice.

When, the following morning, Edgerley's cutlery started to jump up and down on the table, he became seriously concerned. And just as he was frowning into his buttercup tea, a great clod of earth bounced off his shoulder. A second later, a dark and dirty head and shoulders heaved itself up through the floor!

Edgerley was speechless, but the stranger wasn't.

"Who," he cried, "had the idotic idea of putting a house here?"

Edgerley found his voice.
"What are you talking about?

Why are you digging under my house?" he yelled.

The elf could see now that it was a troll glaring at him through the grime. "I'm digging for gold, of course," said the troll in withering tones. "What else would I be doing? Gold is the only thing worth anything at all."

Edgerley sensed that it wasn't worth starting on the "What about rainbows?" conversation. Instead, he ordered the troll to leave at once.

The troll, whose name was Tuggle, refused. For most of the rest of the morning, the argument raged back and forth.

"A troll never gives up when he smells gold," said Tuggle. "And I smell gold right here." He sniffed the air with gruesome glee. "The sooner I can get back to work," he went on, "the sooner I'll be out of your way."

Edgerley thought for a moment. Perhaps there was something in what the troll said. Reluctantly, he agreed.

"Hurry up!" he said. "And don't make too much mess!"

Even Edgerley was impressed by how hard the troll worked. It seemed only fair to give him a drink and some sandwiches at lunchtime.

As the afternoon wore on, Edgerley found himself peering down into the ever-widening hole. It was fascinating seeing all the tree roots, creepy-crawlies and other bits and pieces under the earth. He even began to get a little bit interested in gold.

For the troll talked as he dug, and the way he spoke about the yellow metal made it sound like the most wonderful thing in the world. As night fell, Edgerley lit lanterns so that work could continue. By six o'clock he was down in the hole as well, digging away with his own little spade.

By two in the morning, the elf was as dirty and tired as the troll, but neither of them stopped. When the elf spotted a glint of something in the lamplight, his cry of triumph was just as loud as Tuggle's.

Dawn found Tuggle and Edgerley sitting on the elf's doorstep, sipping buttercup tea and gazing rapturously at a chunk of gold lying on the grass before them.

"I could always use an assistant," said Tuggle.

Edgerley was about to agree when he noticed that the sun was gleaming just as richly on a little patch of buttercups by his door. He looked up at the rosy sky and sighed.

"No," he said, "I'll stay here. But thank you for asking. And good luck!"

After all, the best thing is that there is room in the wide world for both trolls and elves. If there is a pot of gold at the end of every rainbow, maybe there's a rainbow above every pot of gold.

The Ugliest Ogre Contest

All ogres are ugly. They are proud of it. If you tell a young ogre that his mother looks like a toad, he won't smack you on the head with a smelly fish or throw you in a puddle and jump up and down on your middle. He will probably go pink with pleasure and say, "Oh, thanks!"

On the other hand, when a mother ogre shows you her new baby, it's a big mistake to say, "Ooooh! Cootchy, cootchy coo! Isn't he handsome?" You might well find yourself upside down in an ogre-sized bowl of toad-spawn soup.

You will begin to see, now, why the annual Ugliest Ogre Contest was a big event.
Ogres, as you know, have a bad reputation with most elves, and one ogre in the
area was more than enough. But the annual Ugliest Ogre Contest was held in a
different part of the country each year. Each summer, somewhere in Elfland, one
unlucky bunch of elves, going about their business with not a care in the world,
was about to be visited by not one, not two, but hundreds of ogres. This year it
was the town of Umble that drew the short straw.

The first the elves of Umble knew about the Ugliest Ogre Contest was when old
Ma Placket, doing her laundry early one Monday morning, was suddenly terrified
out of her wits by a grinning face at the window. It turned her blood cold and
her washing green. Much to the relief of old Pa Placket, she was unable to speak
for days.

Ma Placket may have been silent, but she pretty soon made sure that everyone knew there were ogres on the loose. By lunchtime, every house had its shutters drawn and its doors barred. No elves stirred on the streets of Umble, but several hundred ogres clomped heavily over the cobblestones with just one thought on their minds: ugliness.

Now ogres are not very competitive. When it comes to running, jumping or throwing anything larger than a pork pie they couldn't care less who is fastest, highest, or hungriest. But when the subject is ugliness, they care very much indeed. All year, the main contenders in the contest had been undergoing rigorous ugliness regimes, aimed at heightening their hideousness.

"They say," an ogre called Glurp told his friend, "that Aaghish George puts a poultice of hedgehog spikes and nettles on his face every day."

"That's nothing," replied Plurk. "Burple Punkt never washes, never combs his hair, and never cuts his nails. My sister thinks he's soooo ugly, she has a picture of him on her wall."

The details of the contest would have horrified the orderly little elves who were still crouching in their houses. You see, ogres are suspicious of anyone telling them what to do. That is why there is no ogre king, or prime minister, or president. They prefer to shamble along in an untidy sort of way, getting what they want mainly by shouting and shaking their fists. It's not that they actually ever come to blows, but a shaking fist is an ugly thing, which is just what ogres like.

So it will not surprise you to know that Ugliest Ogre Contests do not have proper judges or referees with score cards. Instead, members of the audience yell for the ogre they personally find unbelievably unbeautiful. It is a horrible noise and it sometimes goes on for days.

In the meantime, the contestants try to make the ugliest faces they can, which is exhausting. It's as difficult to frown all the time as it is to smile all the time, and some ogre smiles, I fear, are more hideous than any other ogre expression. Anything that shows pointy yellow teeth can't be good, you must admit.

On the day of the contest itself, the ogres gathered in the town square. To get a good view, some of them sat on nearby rooftops, doing serious damage to chimneys in the process. In the middle of the square, on a specially built stage, the contestants strutted their stuff.

First to appear was Aaghish George. "Ugly" doesn't really begin to express the awfulness of his face. One glimpse of it would make you lose your appetite for a month. Two glimpses might finish you off altogether. But the ogres loved it. Admiring murmurs arose from the crowd. Several female ogres fainted. Aaghish George was going to be hard to beat.

But Burple Punkt had a horribleness of features that was quite ghastly. The ogres roared their approval. Burple held his breath until his face turned purple and his eyes almost popped out. The crowd loved it.

There were a few other contestants, of course, but it soon became clear that this was a two-ogre race. Aaghish George and Burple Punkt were the only ones in with a chance. They glared at each other and wiggled their ears.

"The mirror test! The mirror test!" yelled the crowd. It was a well-known ploy at times like this. Sure enough, several elf shops were raided and the large plate-glass mirrors inside were dragged out.

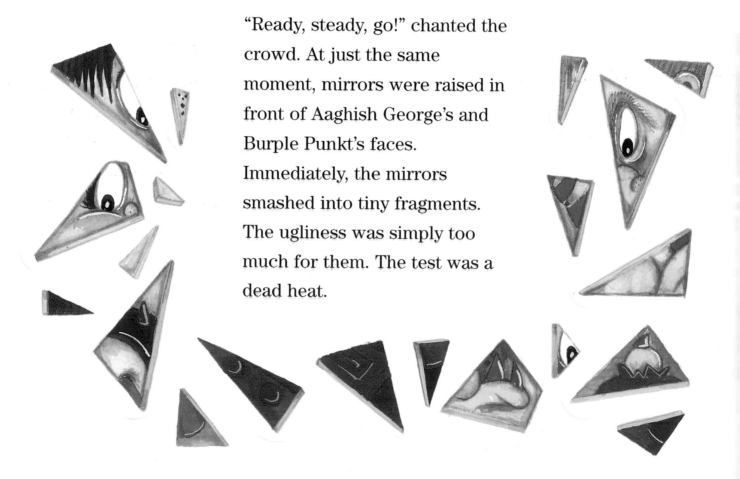

"Ready, steady, go!" chanted the crowd. At just the same moment, mirrors were raised in front of Aaghish George's and Burple Punkt's faces. Immediately, the mirrors smashed into tiny fragments. The ugliness was simply too much for them. The test was a dead heat.

The ugliness was simply too much for them. The test was a dead heat.

Now the watching ogres were yelling so hard they were becoming hoarse.

"Aaghish George! A-a-g-h-i-s-h G-e-o-r-g-e!" shouted one side of the square.

"Burple Punkt! B-u-r-p-l-e P-u-n-k-t!" shouted the other.

"I can't stand this any more," said Ma Placket, barricaded in her kitchen with Pa Placket and her sister's cow. "The sooner this is over, the better. We'll have to get rid of one of the contestants. Then the other will be the clear winner, the ogres will go home, and we can live normal lives again. What we need is a plan."

But as it turned out, Ma Placket didn't need a plan. Five ogres, eager to shout and cheer more loudly decided that the rooftops were not tall enough. Eagerly and clumsily, they began to climb the church steeple—the same church steeple that an elvish engineer had recently shaken his head over.

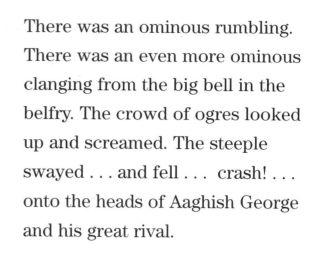

There was an ominous rumbling. There was an even more ominous clanging from the big bell in the belfry. The crowd of ogres looked up and screamed. The steeple swayed . . . and fell . . . crash! . . . onto the heads of Aaghish George and his great rival.

When the dust cleared, the two contestants lay still. There was silence from the crowd. Then a sigh of relief ran through the crowd as first Aaghish George and then Burple Punkt rose from the wreckage.

But the sighs of relief soon turned to sighs of horror. Aaghish George, covered with dirt and twigs and with a weather vane perched on his head, looked uglier than ever. But Burple Punkt had something different on his head— the bell!

It covered his face completely. You couldn't have said he looked beautiful. You couldn't have said he was attractive in any way. But you couldn't have said he was ugly either.

Burple Punkt pulled and tugged. Some extremely ogreish language, unfit for the ears of young elves, came booming out of the bell, but that was all. No face appeared. He was stuck.

There was no doubt about it. Aaghish George was clearly the ugliest ogre present. To the cheers of his supporters, he was carried shoulder-high from the square and out of the town. Poor Burple Punk still booming, was led away as well.

One by one, the elves of Umble crawled out of their homes and viewed the state of their square. It looked awful. But let's face it, compared with dozens of truly hideous ogres, it was absolutely, overwhelmingly . . . gorgeous!